Cock-Ups

Cock–Ups

Simon Moss

faber and faber
LONDON·BOSTON

First published in 1984
by Faber and Faber Limited
3 Queen Square London WC1N 3AU
Filmset by Wilmaset, Birkenhead
Printed in Great Britain by
Redwood Burn Limited, Trowbridge, Wiltshire
All rights reserved

All rights whatsoever in this play are strictly reserved
and applications to perform it, etc., must be made in
advance, before rehearsals begin, to Fraser and
Dunlop (Scripts) Limited of 91 Regent Street, London W1

British Library Cataloguing in Publication Data

Moss, Simon
Cock-ups.
I. Title
821'.914   PR6025.o/
ISBN 0–571–13080–1

Library of Congress Cataloging in Publication Data

Moss, Simon.
Cock-ups: a play.

1. Orton, Joe—Drama.   2. Halliwell, Kenneth—Drama.
I. Title.
PR6063.0833C6   1984   822'.914   83-5555
ISBN 0–571–13080–1 (pbk.)

Characters

KENNETH

JOE

DETECTIVE INSPECTOR TRUSCOTT

RUSSELL

WATSON

CHARLES GENZIANI

MISS MILLIGAN

RICHARD SMART

Cock-Ups was first produced, in a slightly different form, at the Edinburgh Festival in 1981. This version of the play was first performed at the Corn Exchange, Manchester, by the Royal Exchange Theatre Company on 19 April 1983. The cast was as follows:

KENNETH	Patrick Malahide
JOE	Ron Cook
DETECTIVE INSPECTOR TRUSCOTT	Colin McCormack
RUSSELL	Tom Cotcher
WATSON	Max Gold
CHARLES GENZIANI	Christopher Hancock
MISS MILLIGAN	Jean Rimmer
RICHARD SMART	Sean Chapman

Director Greg Hersov
Designer Caroline McCulloch
Lighting Paul W. Jones
Sound John Del'Nero and Jenny Hislop

Set

Three rooms are needed and the action switches from one to another to another with neither hesitation nor delay.

The most important room belongs to Joe and Kenneth. A massive collage dominates its walls and encourages a feeling of claustrophobia. The floor is covered with highly polished linoleum. Such furniture as there is is very simple: a low coffee table from which a slide projector can be angled to face a wall; a queen-size three-quarter bed with built-in drawers; several bookcases; a bedside table; a dressing table; and finally, a desk with a typewriter and reams of paper. There are two doors: one to the corridor, the other to the kitchen.

The other rooms belong to Miss Milligan and Charles Genziani. The available stage space may demand that these rooms may only be suggested; in which case beds, chairs and door-frames are the essential features.

Ideally, these two rooms should be above the former and a staircase should link the two levels.

Slides

A number of slides are relevant to the action:

1 Joe and Kenneth in Morocco.
2 Joe lying on a sun bed, his legs parted for the camera.
3 Joe sitting in the partially decorated flat.
4 Truscott proudly displaying a defaced library book.
5 A scene from *Loot*—Truscott kicking someone to the floor.
6 A mock cast photo for *Entertaining Mr Sloane* with Genziani as Ed, Miss Milligan as Kath, and Smart as Sloane.
7 Morocco—in the foreground Joe and Kenneth are laughing; in the background are two outraged tourists.
8 A place-setting card—'Mr and Mrs Orton'.

These eight slides are the only ones that specifically draw the attention of the characters.

Many others will be required to pass by (without comment) and to be flicked through (with comment). They should be relaxed and informal photos of two people who enjoy each other's company—in this sense the slides should provide a distinct contrast to the onstage action.

ACT ONE

A slide projector, the drum type, clicks on and off in the darkness, showing a variety of slides of JOE *and* KENNETH *on the rear wall of their room. The light from each slide is just sufficient to illuminate* KENNETH, *who stands in his pyjamas, motionless, above the sleeping form of* JOE. *In his tightly clenched fist, a hammer.*

Suddenly the lights rise on the room. The slides stop. KENNETH *is bewildered: this cannot be happening. He sees* JOE *on the bed, his head smashed and his blood spattered on the wall behind. He also sees himself lying dead on the floor. This cannot be happening.*

There is now a pounding at the door—supplied by three anxious people: MISS MILLIGAN, CHARLES GENZIANI *and* RICHARD SMART. KENNETH *is trapped and scared. He presses himself against the wall behind the door to the corridor.*

This cannot be happening.

MILLIGAN: Kenneth? Kenneth? Open the door, Kenneth!

GENZIANI: If you're in there, Joe, let us in.

(*The letter flap is pushed open.*)

SMART: There's someone on the floor.

MILLIGAN: What's he doing?

SMART: Nothing.

MILLIGAN: Let me see.

(*She takes her turn to peer through the flap.*)

Hello, boys, it's only me.

GENZIANI: Oh don't be so stupid.

MILLIGAN: Are you asleep, Kenneth?

SMART: What the hell are they up to?

GENZIANI: There's obviously something seriously wrong here.

SMART: Yeah, but what?

MILLIGAN: Coooee!

GENZIANI: Come away from there.

11

MILLIGAN: I'm only curious.

SMART: I want to know what's happening. That one on the floor don't look well. And where's Joe? What's happened to Joe?

MILLIGAN: I'm not prying, Kenneth, really I'm not.

GENZIANI: I'm sure everything will be quite all right.

(*Two uniformed constables,* WATSON *and* RUSSELL, *come down the corridor.*)

Heavens, you were quick.

WATSON: We're looking for the residence of a Mr Kenneth Halliwell.

GENZIANI: I only phoned two minutes ago.

WATSON: Does he live here?

GENZIANI: Well, yes he does, but . . .

WATSON: Excuse me.

(*He rings the door bell.*)

SMART: We've tried that.

RUSSELL: (*To the gathering*) What are you waiting for?

WATSON: (*Through the letter flap*) Come now, Mr Halliwell, there's no need to barricade yourself in, this is a purely routine visit.

GENZIANI: But we called you.

WATSON: Yes, you're right, of course. It's all right, Mr Halliwell, they called us, so there's even less cause for alarm.

RUSSELL: Not that there was any in the first place.

WATSON: Don't be frightened, Mr Halliwell. Why are you lying on the floor?

SMART: I reckon they're dead.

GENZIANI: Hush, lad.

RUSSELL: Christ, what if we're too late?

WATSON: We're going to have to force the door. Sorry about this, Mr Halliwell. (*To the others*) Stand back.

RUSSELL: Mind that uniform.

(WATSON *takes a run at the door and it bursts open. It swings back and conceals* KENNETH.)

WATSON: Ah. There seems to have been an incident.

(*There is an unseemly rush of people into the room.*)

SMART: Oh God.

(MISS MILLIGAN *promptly faints.* RUSSELL, *the last to enter, now closes the door.* KENNETH *has disappeared, temporarily, from his own nightmare.*)

RUSSELL: They're dead.

WATSON: Let's not be premature. Mr Halliwell, can you hear me?

SMART: (*Deeply shocked*) Joe's dead. Joe's been killed.

WATSON: (*With* KENNETH's *body*) He's playing it tight-lipped: it's a classic case.

RUSSELL: Call the police!

GENZIANI: You are the police.

RUSSELL: Oh God, yes.

WATSON: Shut up, Russell.

SMART: His head. Look at his head. There's nothing there any more.

GENZIANI: (*Next to* SMART) This boy has frozen solid.

(DETECTIVE INSPECTOR TRUSCOTT *walks down the corridor, a piece of paper in his hand, looking for the room to which he has been called. He pauses outside the door and then moves on . . . up the stairs.*)

WATSON: Comfort him, would you?

GENZIANI: (*Doing so with a reassuring arm*) What about Miss Milligan?

WATSON: We'll attend to her.

(*He draws* RUSSELL *to his side and they crouch over the inert* MISS MILLIGAN.)

I wish you'd mind your tongue sometimes. You're forever landing me in it.

RUSSELL: Look, the police are going to be here any minute and we're going to be found with two dead bodies and a receipt from a theatrical costumier. I don't know about you, but I'm all for getting out of here.

WATSON: Hold on, we've done nothing wrong. We're simply

here to ask Mr Halliwell some questions.

RUSSELL: And we're knee-deep in corpses whilst impersonating police officers. I wouldn't fancy our chances in a court of law.

WATSON: (*Slapping* MISS MILLIGAN) Come on, wake up.

RUSSELL: A preliminary psychiatric report, you said . . . well, he's certainly confirmed all our theories, hasn't he? He did take his own life.

WATSON: But the interesting thing is that he took someone else with him.

RUSSELL: Bloody fascinating.

(TRUSCOTT *has arrived at* GENZIANI's *flat. He knocks and waits*.)

WATSON: Have you no intellectual curiosity? This case history could set us up for life.

RUSSELL: Or have us sent *down* for life.

(TRUSCOTT *kicks open* GENZIANI's *door. He is wary and puzzled and searches the room cautiously*.)

What the hell was that?

GENZIANI: There's someone in my room!

SMART: His head's been smashed to smithereens.

WATSON: (*To* RUSSELL) You're inciting mass hysteria, you idiot. Calm down everybody.

(TRUSCOTT *leaves the room upstairs and makes his way down*.)

GENZIANI: There's someone in my room, I tell you.

WATSON: This is no time to get territorial, sir.

GENZIANI: Do something!

RUSSELL: I'm getting out of here.

WATSON: Russell. . . !

RUSSELL: Screw the thesis.

(*He throws open the door and confronts* TRUSCOTT *at the foot of the stairs. He promptly dashes back into the room and slams the door*.)

Hide the bodies!

WATSON: What?

RUSSELL: There's somebody out there.

14

WATSON: Control yourself. Take one of these.

(*Throws him a tablet from* KENNETH's *large jar.*)

RUSSELL: What's this?

WATSON: Swallow it, it'll help.

(TRUSCOTT *knocks on the door.*)

GENZIANI: You're not policemen.

WATSON: If you can't believe your own eyes, sir, that's your own delusion. I'll give you a check-up when I have the time.

(*He opens the door.*)

Yes?

TRUSCOTT: Detective Inspector Truscott of the Yard. I hope you can explain . . .

(*He sees the carnage.*) Sweet Jesus! You (*to* WATSON), get these two out of here. No phone calls, no visitors, no press, and if anyone wants to leave the building, I want their reasons in writing. Jump to it!

(WATSON *has no alternative. He ushers* GENZIANI *and* SMART *out.*)

And you (*to* RUSSELL), take a look out there, see if we've got any more of them. Jesus Christ, what is this place? Charon's waiting-room?

(*And* RUSSELL *similarly has no choice: he goes to the kitchen.*)

Triple murder, eh? Yet another fatal *ménage à trois.*

(RUSSELL *returns.*)

Well?

RUSSELL: A small kitchen and a bathroom.

TRUSCOTT: No more mortal remains?

RUSSELL: No.

TRUSCOTT: Dammit. Never mind, three secures the record for Islington. Touched anything?

RUSSELL: No, sir.

TRUSCOTT: Everything as you found it?

RUSSELL: Yes, sir.

(WATSON, GENZIANI *and* SMART *reach* GENZIANI's *room. They lower* SMART *on to the bed and* WATSON *begins to ask questions.*)

TRUSCOTT: What's your name, lad?

RUSSELL: Russell.

TRUSCOTT: Not used to a bit of blood, eh, Russell?

RUSSELL: Just a bit warm, sir, that's all.

TRUSCOTT: Yes, a beautiful day out there. I would let you open the window, but the place would be full of flies and the path. lab would be on at us about maggots. Loosen your collar if you like.

RUSSELL: Thank you, sir.

TRUSCOTT: We'll be working on this alone for a while. I don't want the forensic paraphernalia clod-hopping around and messing us about. Right then, let's get down to business. (*He shakes his head.*) What a mess. Makes you wonder what the world's coming to. (*Notebook out.*) Cause of death . . . (JOE) . . . number of blows to the head with heavy, blunt object. And still fairly warm. (*And now* KENNETH) This one's been dead a while —stone-cold. (MISS MILLIGAN) And she's still warm enough to roast chestnuts by. This is most perplexing. Any ideas, constable?

RUSSELL: Er . . . there's this.

TRUSCOTT: What's that?

RUSSELL: (*Reaching beside* KENNETH *for it*) A diary. (*Reading the note on top of it*) 'If you read this all will be explained,' signed KH. And, 'PS Especially the latter part.' The inevitable suicide note.

TRUSCOTT: (*Taking both*) From all three of them, constable? (*To* RUSSELL*'s dismay he turns over the note but throws away the diary.*)
If I read this all will be explained, will it? (*Reading*) 'Bread, milk, wine, grapefruit juice, eggs? Tomatoes, onions, mince, pasta, peppers, Parmesan . . . nembutal . . . *Doctor Faustus* . . .' If I read this, all will be explained? I'm used to more illuminating last words than these. (*Throws the note.*) Here, have a hunt about, see what you can find.

RUSSELL: (*Gesturing at* MISS MILLIGAN) But . . . well . . .
shouldn't I get her a drink?

TRUSCOTT: A stiff one, I imagine.
(*He permits himself a chuckle.*)

RUSSELL: Some water.

TRUSCOTT: We only read rights, we don't administer them.
(*He is humouring* RUSSELL.) Get her wet and everyone will
think she drowned. No, I can appreciate any religious
beliefs you may cherish, but you would be foolish to
expect any kind of resurrection. Off you go, lad.
(*Once more,* RUSSELL *has no option.* TRUSCOTT *seats himself on
the edge of the bed, moving* JOE's *legs to do so.*)
If only you could talk, old son. Who clobbered you, eh?
(*He becomes aware he is sitting on something. He discovers a
long, heavy phallus.*)
Bugger me sideways!

RUSSELL: Sir?

TRUSCOTT: Explore the possibilities of such a device!

RUSSELL: Is that an order, sir?

TRUSCOTT: This is the most offensive weapon I've ever seen.

RUSSELL: Could it be a murder weapon, though?

TRUSCOTT: It's certainly no seed drill. Keep looking,
constable. See what other primitive artefacts have been
secreted. (*Produces a plastic bag for it.*) This case could be
my finest hour, constable. My name in the headlines,
syndication—the fame I've always deserved! They'll
realize then what a great talent has been hidden, they'll
know what they've been missing all these years, all
those years of second fiddle . . .
(TRUSCOTT *dries up.* MISS MILLIGAN *is struggling to her feet.*)
A miracle!

RUSSELL: (*Tactfully*) Sir . . .
(TRUSCOTT *silences him with a raised finger.*)

MILLIGAN: (*Delirious*) Oooh, I feel all woozy.

TRUSCOTT: Can we accept testimony from the dead?

MILLIGAN: What a mess you boys have left this place in.

17

RUSSELL: You've made rather a loose assumption, sir . . .

MILLIGAN: It's not like you to be untidy, Kenneth.

(*She is at the door.*)

TRUSCOTT: We must follow her. This is quite uncanny.

MILLIGAN: (*At the stairs*) Would you like to come upstairs until I've cleaned up?

TRUSCOTT: (*Following*) She's calling us. (*As* MISS MILLIGAN *climbs*) I'll confess, I always thought ascensions were more spectacular than this.

(*The lights have faded on the room.*)

MILLIGAN: We'll have a nice chat over a cup of tea.

(*She is almost out of sight.*)

TRUSCOTT: (*To* RUSSELL) Keep up now.

RUSSELL: (*At the foot of the stairs*) There's something you ought to know, sir.

(MISS MILLIGAN *enters her room.* RUSSELL *climbs the stairs after* TRUSCOTT. TRUSCOTT *enters her room and stands framed by the doorway.*)

TRUSCOTT: Can this really be Heaven?

(*There is a commotion in the corridor as the lights fade on this room.*

KENNETH *rushes down, opens the door to the flat and dashes inside. He slams the door shut and leans his weight against it, breathless. The lights on, we can see that the room has reverted to its state the evening before: no blood, no bodies.*

JOE, *with two large bags of groceries, has now reached the front door.*)

JOE: Kenneth? Kenneth? Open the door, Kenneth!

(*They are both laughing.*)

If you don't open this door, Kenneth Halliwell, I shall batter you senseless with a large bag of groceries!

KENNETH: Such empty threats.

JOE: You think I'm joking? I'm warning you . . .

KENNETH: You'll never take me alive, copper.

JOE: I'll take you over the kitchen table if you don't open this door!

KENNETH: Nope.

JOE: Come on, Kenneth.

(*No answer.* JOE *begins to tire of the game.*)

Kenneth.

KENNETH: Sorry.

JOE: Kenneth!

(*He finally opens the door.*)

Thank you.

(*Enters.*)

Where do you want this lot?

KENNETH: Just dump it anywhere.

(JOE *drops them at the foot of the bed and collapses.*)

JOE: Ah . . . chez nous.

KENNETH: Home sweet homosexual.

(JOE *exhales and relaxes.*)

JOE: Thank Christ today is over and done with.

KENNETH: Never mind.

(*He sits at the end of the bed, moving* JOE*'s legs to do so.*)

Right.

(*Begins to sort through bags.*)

What have we forgotten?

JOE: Throw the biscuits.

KENNETH: (*Doing so*) You'll spoil supper.

JOE: No, I won't, I'm only having a couple.

(*He gets up and goes to his desk where he reads a sheaf of notes.*)

KENNETH: You know what we did forget?

JOE: (*Offhand*) What's that?

KENNETH: Only the fucking Parmesan.

JOE: It doesn't matter.

KENNETH: Of course it matters. It's fucked up the whole meal before I've even started.

JOE: I can easily go without a sprinkling of cheese.

KENNETH: It wouldn't be the same. (*Easy come, easy go*) I'll have to do something else.

JOE: Okay.

19

KENNETH: But what?

JOE: What else did you get?

KENNETH: Nothing else. I'm so stupid . . .

JOE: Sandwich.

KENNETH: Well, that's not a meal, is it?

JOE: It'll suit me, I don't mind. Do whatever's easiest for you.

KENNETH: I've got some ham.

JOE: Sure.

KENNETH: Or there's some liver sausage left.

JOE: No.

KENNETH: Or I've got some pilchards.

JOE: Urgh. Ham.

KENNETH: How many rounds?

JOE: I don't know . . . two? For the time being.

KENNETH: Anything on them?

JOE: No.

KENNETH: (*Rummaging in bags*) I even put it on the list.

JOE: I'm happy with a sandwich.

(KENNETH *throws his library book from the bag to the head of the bed. A bottle of tablets follows.*)

KENNETH: Nothing you want out of here, is there?

JOE: I don't know, is there?

KENNETH: No. Shall I open this wine?

JOE: If you like.

KENNETH: Are you going to have any?

JOE: If you are, yes.

KENNETH: I thought I might have a glass.

JOE: I'll have one with you.

KENNETH: I won't open it if you don't want me to.

JOE: What? Kenneth, it's a cheap bottle of plonk, not bloody Pandora's Box: open it if you want to.

KENNETH: It seems silly to open it if we're not going to finish it.

JOE: I expect, between the two of us, we can finish it one way or another.

KENNETH: Just checking.

JOE: Making Matterhorns out of molehills.

KENNETH: Sorry.

JOE: Go on, open the wine. Let's have a party.

(*He makes a silly face at* KENNETH. *They both smile. But as* KENNETH *turns away,* KENNETH*'s smile evaporates. The lights fade on the flat and rise on* MISS MILLIGAN*'s room.* RUSSELL *has just broken the news to* TRUSCOTT.)

TRUSCOTT: What do you mean: she only fainted?

RUSSELL: She just saw the bodies and went over—CRASH.

TRUSCOTT: Why didn't you tell me before?

RUSSELL: I did try.

(MISS MILLIGAN *crosses the room with a bucket and mop.*)

MILLIGAN: Hello, Inspector.

TRUSCOTT: Don't you 'Hello, Inspector' me, you charlatan. Lying there playing possum with your skirts above your knees.

MILLIGAN: Were you peeping?

TRUSCOTT: Legs crazed with veins like a hunk of Stilton, you've got. Those two men are dead. What have you to say in your defence?

MILLIGAN: I've never known Kenneth to make a mess.

TRUSCOTT: If you are pleading insanity, madam, we will need a far more rational statement than this.

MILLIGAN: All that blood. Well, really, Inspector, it's not like him.

TRUSCOTT: May I ask what you were doing last night, *Miss* Milligan?

MILLIGAN: I was sleeping, Inspector.

TRUSCOTT: Can anyone substantiate your story?

MILLIGAN: Why, no, I was alone.

TRUSCOTT: I see. What exactly were you doing then?

MILLIGAN: Sleeping after half-past ten. I always go to sleep after half-past ten. That's how I keep my youthful good looks.

TRUSCOTT: The nocturnal habits of *elderly* spinsters are

21

naturally unknown to me. Now, I realize that you must be very upset at the loss of your two dear friends but you will understand that I must exploit this weakness and ask you some questions.

MILLIGAN: By all means.

TRUSCOTT: How long had they lived here?

MILLIGAN: Oh, years and years. We've become one great, big happy family.

TRUSCOTT: Like the Krays, you mean.

MILLIGAN: We do lots of things together.

TRUSCOTT: Yes, I'm sure.

MILLIGAN: Tea. Conversation. Chatter and gossip. Little things. (*Picking fluff from his lapel*) You need a woman's touch, Inspector.

TRUSCOTT: I've had one, madam. It was expensive and overrated. I gather from what you say and from your general appearance that you cleaned for them.

MILLIGAN: Oh no.

TRUSCOTT: An au pair, then. Particularly fashionable at the moment is the leggy, foreign bint doing the housework.

MILLIGAN: That's Kenneth's province: the housework. He makes that lino gleam. I'm often scared of entering in a dress in case the reflection from the floor lets the boys see my secrets.

RUSSELL: She's refusing to accept their deaths, sir. It's a common enough condition—the bereaved will deliberately cultivate a sensation of presence.

TRUSCOTT: (*Eyeing him strangely*) Thank you, constable. Most informative. I wonder . . . (*To* MISS MILLIGAN) Do you know what this is?

(*He produces the phallus.*)

MILLIGAN: (*Squinting*) A truncheon?

TRUSCOTT: Come now, Miss Milligan.

MILLIGAN: A silly vanity, Inspector, I'm not wearing my glasses.

TRUSCOTT: (*Brandishing it in her face*) Does this help?

MILLIGAN: (*Shocked*) Oooh!

TRUSCOTT: You know what it is then?

MILLIGAN: Yes.

TRUSCOTT: And you won't be wanting another glass of water?

MILLIGAN: Simply because I never took a husband does not mean that I am ignorant of the ways of the world. That was Joe's.

TRUSCOTT: Joe's?

MILLIGAN: He brought it back with him from Africa. Kenneth told me that you can buy them in England. In plastic.

TRUSCOTT: The totem of an ethnic culture but hardly a souvenir. Duty-free tobacco and castanets are one thing . . . did they ever, to your knowledge, use this thing?

MILLIGAN: Well, it's not the kind of thing that one likes to talk about.

TRUSCOTT: I find that depends a great deal upon the company one keeps. (*He thinks.*) A symbol of fertility that deals savage death. I do not like this one bit. I do not like the idea of two men having one of these.
(*The lights fade on this room and rise on the flat below.* KENNETH *stands as before.* JOE *reaches for the tablet bottle. He reads its label.*)

JOE: Are these any good?

KENNETH: (*Preoccupied*) What?

JOE: These nembutals.
(KENNETH *'wakes'. He gathers up the groceries.*)

KENNETH: They scramble my preconscious, shuffle my unconscious and (*as he goes*) I think they're giving me breasts.

JOE: Lovely.
(KENNETH *goes to the kitchen.* JOE *seeks out* KENNETH*'s large jar of pills. He drops the nembutals in one by one.*)
You've got more tablets than Moses. (*He runs out of*

tablets finally.) Have you seen the slides from last
    night, Ken?

KENNETH: Sorry?

JOE: The slides in the blue box.

KENNETH: Are they on the bookcase? Third shelf down?

JOE: (*Looking*) Yep. Got them.

KENNETH: Haven't you finished that yet?

JOE: You can't rush a pocket autobiography, Kenneth,
    certainly not with a life like mine. Hey! Did you take
    those biscuits out there with you?

KENNETH: I'm doing you sandwiches.

JOE: I just want something to tide me over.
    (*He checks something in his notes on the desk.*)

KENNETH: I thought you were meant to be going out tonight.

JOE: This has got to go to press by Friday.

KENNETH: What about Roger?

JOE: Bugger Roger.

KENNETH: I thought that was the whole intention.

JOE: Ha-ha-ha. No, I want to get this done and out of the
    way. It's been hanging round my neck for too long.
    (*A loud crash from the kitchen.*)

KENNETH: (*Coming in*) Fucking hell!

JOE: What's wrong now?

KENNETH: You want a fucking Buddha to wait on you hand
    and foot, you do, not me. I've dropped the bloody lot.
    Look at me, I'm sodden.
    (*There is a splash of water down his leg.*)

JOE: (*Laughing*) You look as if you've wet yourself. You're
    getting incontinent in your old age.

KENNETH: Thank you.

JOE: Come on, I'll give you a hand.
    (*The lights fade on them and rise on* MISS MILLIGAN*'s room.*
    MISS MILLIGAN *is just leaving with her bucket and mop.*)

RUSSELL: Where do you think you're going?
    (WATSON *enters past her.*)

WATSON: Leave her, we've got to talk.

RUSSELL: I was told to guard her.

WATSON: You know who the other dead bloke is, don't you?

RUSSELL: Joe someone.

WATSON: Only bloody Joe Orton.

RUSSELL: Joe Orton?

WATSON: Christ, you must have heard of him. Writes plays.

RUSSELL: No.

WATSON: He's dead famous.

RUSSELL: What an unfortunate choice of words.

WATSON: The point is that Halliwell lived with him. I've been getting all this from the bloke next door.

RUSSELL: The one Truscott's gone to see?

WATSON: The thing is that if Halliwell was living in the shadow of Orton then we've got a best seller on our hands. The first thesis to be published in the *News of the World*!

RUSSELL: It was intellectual curiosity a while ago, now it's financial gain. I say we should cut our losses and get out while we still can. If this Orton is as famous as you say he is then we're really going to cop it.

WATSON: Where's the glory in conservatism? The meek certainly don't inherit kidney-shaped swimming pools and Aston Martins. We could bring psychiatry out from under the couches.

RUSSELL: You can't commercialize the mental sciences.

WATSON: Think of Halliwell, though . . . he's been prescribed every sedative in the book and still he batters Orton's brains out. Now that's quite something. There's closeted sexuality, frustrated passions, inadequacy and insecurity, injured narcissism . . . this is the stuff of real life, baby.

RUSSELL: I don't know how to expect to psychoanalyse a corpse. We dressed up as policemen to put him at his ease—he'll answer questions to a uniform, you said—and that obviously hasn't worked. Now what are you going to do? One knock for yes, two knocks for no:

is there anybody there?

WATSON: Well you won't learn your trade with your head stuck in books all day—you've got to get out and probe the subconscious of the man in the street.

RUSSELL: Even if he is stretched out on the floor.

WATSON: Go then, I don't care.

RUSSELL: You don't either, do you?

WATSON: Take a look at this place, there's a whole library of theses just waiting to be written. This is a goldmine of clinical madness.

(*The lights fade on them and rise on* GENZIANI's *room.* SMART *is face-down on the bed and* GENZIANI *is gently massaging his back.* TRUSCOTT *is not very happy.*)

TRUSCOTT: And I tell you there is no such thing as sympathetic rigor mortis. What are you trying to hide?

GENZIANI: The boy is near inflexible with grief, and at this range the gnashing of teeth is positively deafening.

TRUSCOTT: I can't hear anything, and if you ask me a body rub is a fitting form of neither therapy nor mourning.

SMART: (*Horizontal*) My muscles tense up. There's nothing I can do about my physiology. I may look all right from where you're standing, but underneath all this clothing, I'm as rigid as a tent pole.

TRUSCOTT: Then you must be some kind of medical freak. I hope you're not taking advantage of this good Samaritan.

SMART: Would I?

TRUSCOTT: The stench of red herrings is quite overpowering. You talk about grief but lie on your stomach virtually twitching with delight. The woman next door babbles on like a lunatic. I am not happy with this case at all. Appearances are not what they appear to be. A room like an abattoir and it has to be me to clear it up!

(*The lights fade on them and rise on the flat below.* MISS MILLIGAN *has just finished washing down the walls and all we see of her work is the final wringing of a blood-stained cloth into the bucket. The room is now clean and tidy and she is rightly pleased with her work. The bodies have been unceremoniously stacked on a trolley, where they lie in state with dusters and polish, etc. With a final flick of her duster over the desk, she wheels the bodies out of the room and down the corridor. She closes the door. Just as it closes* KENNETH *enters from the kitchen. He is puzzled and goes to the front door and opens it to look down the corridor.* JOE *enters from the kitchen with the sandwiches, one of which he is eating.*)

JOE: What are you up to?

KENNETH: (*Wheeling round*) What? Nothing. I thought I heard someone out there.

JOE: You're imagining things. What with that and your shakes.

KENNETH: Yes, you're probably right.
(*He holds out his hand to display the shaking.*)
Look at that.

JOE: (*Genuinely*) Hey, that's quite bad.

KENNETH: I know. I feel as if I ought to be playing the piano.
(*He mimes and* JOE *laughs.*)

JOE: You look like a Thunderbirds puppet.

KENNETH: Oh, very funny. Did you bring the wine?

JOE: I was carrying these.
(*He bites into a sandwich.*)

KENNETH: Hang on then.
(JOE *mimes being hanged.*)
We are on form, aren't we?

JOE: You know me, Ken, every one liable to open up an old appendix scar.
(KENNETH *has collected the wine from the kitchen.*)
Ah, Halliwell, you're here at last. I feared your vulcanized undergarments had led you into private ecstasy somewhere.

KENNETH: I haven't known ecstasy since my hairline receded.
(*Pouring the wine*) The sparkling diuretic you ordered, sir.

JOE: Please remember when waiting on table: always serve

27

from the left and flaunt the arse, the latter being
especially important for it enlivens even the weakest of
appetites.

(*Pats* KENNETH's *bottom*.)

You have a great future behind you, boy.

KENNETH: (*With a squeal*) Sir John! Surely such a flagrant
disregard for table manners will jeopardize your entry
in Burke's *Peerage*?

JOE: Debrett says it is perfectly permissible to fumble one's
waiter providing one uses the finger bowl afterwards,
and this, of course, is standard practice in the House of
Lords. The serving classes are abused between the first,
second, third, fourth and fifth courses in keeping with
tradition. Allow me to violate your alimentary canal by
means of an entrée. I pay at competitive rates and as
well as my entry in Burke's *Peerage*, I am also the
subject of some adulation in Gray's *Anatomy*.

(*He reaches out for* KENNETH, *who neatly sidesteps*.)

KENNETH: It's too hot, Joe.

JOE: You didn't say that in Morocco.

KENNETH: Not now, Joe.

JOE: (*Arms raised in apology*) Sorry. Forgive me. *Peccavi*.

KENNETH: So my influence hasn't been for nothing after all.

JOE: *Peccavi?* It was one of the first words you said to me.
That's Greek to me, I said. Latin, you said.

KENNETH: I have sinned.

JOE: I wonder what you'd done to say that. . . ?

KENNETH: I dread to think.

JOE: I can't quite remember the context . . .

KENNETH: Thank God.

JOE: But it seemed to fit.

KENNETH: With me it always fits.

JOE: And if the cap fits . . .

TOGETHER: (*An old joke*) . . . you're screwing a Dutch
schoolboy!

(*They laugh*.)

KENNETH: Lovely. Those were the days. Life was simple.
(JOE *gently shakes his head and smiles as he recalls a memory: a funny, happy memory.*)
Do you want to make a start?

JOE: Um? Oh, right, yes. Here, drop them in.
(*He gives* KENNETH *the slides to fit into the projector. He goes to the standard lamp and switches it on. He turns off the main light.*)

KENNETH: Romantic.

JOE: *Le mot juste.*

KENNETH: Our own little slide show.

JOE: Better than *Bums* any day.

KENNETH: *Bums* to you. To the cinematic cognoscente, the title of Miss Ono's film is *Bottoms*.

JOE: Ono onan yoyo—bottoms bums arses . . . what's the difference? Give me the real thing.

KENNETH: But not necessarily Roger.

JOE: He'll find someone else to go with. The sooner this is done the better. The whole lot from beginning to end. From the womb to the top!

KENNETH: (*Groaning at the pun*) Dreadful. Blue pencil the entire thing.

JOE: I shall include everything.

KENNETH: I'd happily ghost-write it for you.

JOE: Everything.

KENNETH: Might that not be a little foolish?

JOE: Everything, Kenneth, everything and not a word less.

KENNETH: Surely not on the Sabbath.

JOE: They'll pick up their *Sunday Telegraphs* from the parquet flooring by the front door, they'll open them up in their favourite armchairs and—WHALLOP—everything! The day of rest revelation that the golden boy of the West End . . .

KENNETH: (*Lighting one of many cigarettes*) Queen of the demi-monde.

JOE: . . . is frequently engaged in public lavatories.

KENNETH: And all for the price of a penny. What value this man represents!

JOE: Edna Welthorpe writes . . . 'My husband had just finished his half of the prize crossword when he turned over to read of that young man's abhorrent practices. We have read and reread the article and we still do not understand the significance of the squat thrusts. Now, we do not consider ourselves prudes, our son is a social worker and often helps coloured people . . .'

KENNETH: You'd wallow in that, wouldn't you.

JOE: I might even write it.

KENNETH: No, it's all very bold and pioneering but it's sudden death.

JOE: You'd be there as well.

KENNETH: Is that so?

JOE: Playwright, Joe Orton, a vivacious thirty-four, writes frankly of life in the arms of his personal secretary: 'Looking back over my meteoric rise, I realize that none of this would have been possible were it not for the opportunity to bonk Kenneth Halliwell when the going got tough!' (*Slight pause*) Well? What do you think?

KENNETH: I am not your personal secretary.

JOE: I was only joking.

(KENNETH *reaches into his pill jar and searches for the pill he wants. He finds it and swallows it with wine.*)

Come on, Kenneth.

KENNETH: I'm all right, it's this heat.

JOE: Are you hot?

KENNETH: Aren't you?

JOE: Not especially.

KENNETH: I'm boiling.

JOE: Do you want me to open a window?

KENNETH: What? No . . . the temptation to throw myself out might prove too great.

JOE: (*Laughing, admonishing gently*) Kenneth. (*Stock German psychiatrist voice*) Zo how long hav you been harbouring zeze zuicidal tendenzies, Mr Halliwell?

KENNETH: Oooh . . . about sixteen years, two months and twenty-one days.

JOE: (*Laughing*) But who'ze counting, hah?

KENNETH: (*Smiling*) Let's make a start on this.

JOE: You're going to help me, are you?

KENNETH: If that's all right. I mean, I've been helping you for sixteen years, two months and . . .

JOE: And twenty-one days. Yes, I know.

KENNETH: Why end a successful partnership? As the source material for *all* of your characters, I feel I'm entitled to contribute as often as need be. How far have you got?

JOE: I've just made mention of our collaborations.

KENNETH: Collaborations?

JOE: It's a euphemism.

KENNETH: (*Playing to the joke*) Ah.

JOE: No, all I've done is mentioned our few abortive attempts at literary fame with those no-hope novels.

KENNETH: I thought some of them were rather good.

JOE: That's what I thought at the time. Anyway, all above-board so far, Ken, nothing that's going to get us prosecuted. (*Clicks his fingers*) Valium!

(KENNETH *passes them to him.*)

Thanks. (*Swallowing them*) Nectar.

KENNETH: The ambrosia of the excitable.

JOE: By appointment to the gods.

(*The first slide:* JOE *and* KENNETH *in Morocco.*)

KENNETH: Our first magical, mystery tour.

JOE: How old is this? (*Laughs*) Kenneth, look at that wig!

KENNETH: It's not a very flattering angle.

JOE: Look at it! I adore the two-tone effect. Piebald!

KENNETH: (*Flatly*) You said it suited me perfectly.

JOE: (*As an excuse*) We were young.

KENNETH: I've never been young.

JOE: Christ, Kenneth, it looks like an untrimmed snatch. (*Laughs again.*)

31

KENNETH: (*Dry*) Thank you very much.

JOE: Well, really . . .

KENNETH: Thanks very much, Joe, that's typically thoughtful of you.

JOE: (*Calming himself down*) Sorry . . . sorry. I can get away with mentioning holidaying in Morocco, can't I? I think I'd better leave it at that.

KENNETH: Nothing about the golden land where the boys are accommodating and one can get 'brown' in minutes?

JOE: Tempting, isn't it?

KENNETH: (*Dryly*) It is if you fancy Reading Gaol for your next holiday.

(*The second slide:* JOE *lying on a sun bed with legs spread to the camera.*)

JOE: (*Laughing again*) Oh dear. We're really finding them tonight.

KENNETH: And that's what I call a flattering camera angle!

JOE: What do you reckon? It might make a nice photo to go with the column.

KENNETH: Column being the operative word.

JOE: The coming attraction, perhaps?

KENNETH: I think not, Joe. (*Beat*) Mind you, I enjoyed taking it.

JOE: Out of order, Halliwell, you're beginning to sound like a homosexual. That was totally uncalled for.

KENNETH: As was the brazen posture adopted.

JOE: And the next one please!

(*The third slide:* JOE *sitting on the bed in a partially decorated flat.*)

KENNETH: You could mention moving in here.

JOE: And have a well-beaten trail from all the public bogs in Greater London to our front door? No, thank you. I like to exercise some choice in who I have sex with.

KENNETH: Not a lot, but some.

JOE: There'd be a queue a mile long of manicured old window dressers all wanting to touch a celebrity.

KENNETH: You flatter yourself.

JOE: You'd have to make them tea while they waited.

KENNETH: Ha!

JOE: I shall mention that I live comfortably in a select part of the metropolis.

KENNETH: You can't get much more select than Islington. It's a queers' graveyard. We all come here and wait to die.

JOE: Better here than in some cottage in the country. I'm urban.

KENNETH: You're about as urbane as a drain cleaner.

JOE: You're getting deaf in your old age. Urban! Town dweller.

KENNETH: I wish you'd shut up about my age. And as for urban—you prefer shitty little cubicles to wide, open spaces.

JOE: It's the stuff of real life, baby: there's gold in them thar cubicles.

(*The fourth slide:* TRUSCOTT *holding up a library book.*)

You're fucking nicked, my old beauty!

KENNETH: And weren't we just? The bastard. Six rotten months.

JOE: Ah, you see? I survived my Reading Gaol. Yes, I can use this. It's back to the old business of attitudes to authority again but they love reading about that—it confirms all their worst fears: anarchy; the criminal record; the unpleasant subject matter; the bad language . . .

KENNETH: Yes, you've certainly cultivated your image.

JOE: (*Indignant*) I haven't cultivated it. That's what I'm like, that's the way I am.

(KENNETH *shifts almost in disgust.*)

I am!

KENNETH: No . . .

JOE: What do you mean, no?

KENNETH: Pardon me for saying, but you're trendy, that's all.

JOE: Trendy? Like a floral tie is trendy?

KENNETH: That'd be the sort of thing—new, loud, cheap and ultimately vulgar.

JOE: (*Raising his glass*) Cheers.

KENNETH: The North London 'penthouse', the criminal record—shows you'll go to gaol for your principles—the deprived childhood . . . it's the same old rags to rich-rags story.

JOE: Well, isn't it?

KENNETH: (*Almost sneering*) The victim gets his revenge on society!

JOE: That's what I'm doing.

KENNETH: Who isn't shuffling to London with that load on their backs these days? To the streets paved with gold.

JOE: As you know, in my case it happens to be true.

KENNETH: And you make your money and then that's it. Elocution lessons? Soirées with John, Paul, George and Ringo—the Fab Four? You're really kicking the Establishment between the legs.

JOE: I'm sorry . . . how did we get on to this?

KENNETH: You're only tickling their arses with a feather. There's no revenge left in you, you've left yourself behind. The empty shell of Joe Orton: farceur and ever so outré.

JOE: I wish I knew what you're talking about.

KENNETH: If only you'd listened to me . . .

JOE: I'm listening to you now but I'm not sure I understand a word of it.

KENNETH: (*Changing tack easily*) More wine?

JOE: (*Warily*) Thanks.

(JOE *holds out his glass.* KENNETH *smiles and does the same.* JOE *realizes that he is expected to go to the kitchen for another bottle.*)

KENNETH: It's not often I ask you to do something for me. The exercise will do you good.

(JOE *goes to the kitchen.* KENNETH *lies back on the bed. He*

34

*closes his eyes. He will stay here through the next scenes
until the return of* JOE.

The lights fade on him and rise on MISS MILLIGAN*'s room. The
bodies of* JOE *and* KENNETH *are propped up in chairs and* MISS
MILLIGAN *is offering round tea and biscuits.*)

WATSON: I really don't think Mr Orton can eat much more,
Miss Milligan.

MILLIGAN: Of course he can, he likes his biscuits.

WATSON: (*To* RUSSELL) I'm frightened to stop her, it would
only traumatize her further.

RUSSELL: We've got to do something, this is the third pack of
garibaldi she's stuffed down his throat.

MILLIGAN: (*To the body of* JOE) Go on, just one more.

RUSSELL: And what's the Inspector going to say when he
finds them up here?

WATSON: Try to stop her for a minute—I'll do some serious
thinking.

(*She is raising the tea cup to* KENNETH*'s lips.*)

RUSSELL: Please, Miss Milligan.

MILLIGAN: You're quiet today, Kenneth.

RUSSELL: He deserves to be left to rest in peace.

MILLIGAN: (*Confiding to* RUSSELL) He is a quiet man but you
know what they say about still waters. Kenneth runs
ever so deep. Don't you, Kenneth?

WATSON: (*Mutters*) Six feet under.

RUSSELL: Watson!

WATSON: Well, silly cow.

RUSSELL: As a mental scientist you're meant to be
understanding.

WATSON: Can't you keep her quiet?

RUSSELL: How?

WATSON: I don't know.

MILLIGAN: (*To the body of* KENNETH) Open the tunnel, here
comes the choo-choo.

(RUSSELL *animates* KENNETH*'s body in a desperate and
grotesque ventriloquism act.*)

RUSSELL: (*As* KENNETH) I'm really not terribly hungry.

MILLIGAN: You won't grow up big and strong like Joe.

RUSSELL: (*As* KENNETH, *warming to performance*) I have no desire to grow up like Joe. Take those wretched biscuits away from me, woman.

MILLIGAN: Do you want one of your pills?

RUSSELL: (*As* KENNETH) No thank you.

MILLIGAN: You know what you're like without your pills . . .

(*This attracts* WATSON's *attention*.)

. . . you get all hot and bothered. Not that the pills seem to be doing the job these days, if you ask me.

WATSON: See, I was right about him overriding them. Go on, see what else you can find out.

(*He nudges* RUSSELL *eagerly*.)

MILLIGAN: You ought to see a different doctor: all those pills, it's not right. All day long—pills, pills and they're not getting rid of your pains. (*To* WATSON) He gets terrible stomach pains. So much for the National Health Service. (*To* 'KENNETH') There's a friend of mine, Kenneth, who's been waiting eighteen months, eighteen months! to have a bunion removed. Eighteen months! It's not right.

WATSON: Pains. These would be guilt pains—he's been suppressing his aggression and his unconscious has turned it against himself. Fascinating.

MILLIGAN: You know what you need, don't you? Fresh air. You should get out a bit more instead of moping around. It's not Joe's fault he has meetings but if you went out in the evenings now and again, you never know, you might meet a nice young lady. It's never too late to get married, Kenneth. Touch wood. Another biscuit?

RUSSELL: (*As* KENNETH) Not for me. I'm on a diet.

MILLIGAN: On a diet? Why, there's nothing of you. You'll waste away.

WATSON: The chances of that are higher than you think.

RUSSELL: (*As himself*) Watson, can I take my hands off this body? There's something unholy about mobilizing a corpse.

WATSON: Just a few more questions and then we'll get them back downstairs. Ask her about his creative ambitions. I want to know what his imagination was up to—let's try to isolate some classifiable symbols . . .

(*The lights fade on them and rise on* GENZIANI'*s room. The massage continues.*)

GENZIANI: You've looked after your body, haven't you, lad?

SMART: A job like mine, I've got to maintain my appearance.

GENZIANI: Yes, yes, quite . . . easily get out of condition sitting in a car all day. Get flabby. Run to seed. Puff up. The physique of a bean bag.

SMART: Can you go a bit lower?

GENZIANI: You just give the word.

(*He rubs lower, around the waist.*)

Do you use anything special on your skin?

SMART: Baby lotion. Saves me from cracking up.

GENZIANI: Keep yourself smooth and supple, eh?

SMART: Yeah.

GENZIANI: That leather must chafe.

SMART: There you have it.

GENZIANI: You've got a good, strong body: muscular and powerful, yet sleek and streamlined—like a seal. A nice skin balm would enhance your appearance, make you glisten.

SMART: You've put your finger on my style.

GENZIANI: I'm a good judge of character, one look was enough for me. And you care as well, don't you? You care about people.

SMART: (*Sadly*) Joe.

GENZIANI: A tragedy. A man in his prime. You cared about him, I can appreciate that.

SMART: He was a good bloke.

GENZIANI: You miss him?

37

SMART: I will do.

GENZIANI: Well, if you ever need a shoulder to cry on, you just come to me. Tears are nothing to be ashamed of—they're the raindrops of a compassionate nature.
(*He lets his fingers pitter-patter on* SMART's *back.*)

SMART: I was meant to be picking him up.

GENZIANI: Your boss'll understand. He won't expect you to turn up with a corpse under your arm.

SMART: He's a hard man.

GENZIANI: I'll have a little chat with the Inspector. See if you can't be on your way so that you can mourn in private. Chin up, lad.
(*The lights fade on them and rise on the downstairs flat. The door is open and* RUSSELL *and* WATSON *struggle in with the body of* JOE.)

WATSON: Shock has given that woman the strength of ten men.
(*They swing the body on to the bed.*)
Jesus Christ.

RUSSELL: (*Rubbing his groin*) That's hurt me, you know, I'm not used to heavy lifting.

WATSON: (*Looking round*) She's washed the walls down. This is quite incredible—she's obviously carrying on as normal. This is the most detailed instance of repressed bereavement that I've ever heard of.

RUSSELL: What does a hernia feel like?

WATSON: Don't start that, we've got to get Halliwell down yet . . .
(*The door is kicked shut by* TRUSCOTT *who has been hiding behind it.*)

RUSSELL: (*Panic*) We can explain.

TRUSCOTT: You must make your peace with God, not with me, His humble servant.
(*He walks up to* WATSON.)
You're a clever little chap, aren't you?

WATSON: (*Modestly*) Thank you, sir.

TRUSCOTT: Almost too clever for a policeman, it might be said.

WATSON: I'm quite stupid really.

TRUSCOTT: (*To* RUSSELL) And what about you?

RUSSELL: Me? I'm as thick as mud. Thicker in many ways.

TRUSCOTT: (*Pacing*) Is this your manor?

WATSON: Our manner? What . . . bedside manner?

TRUSCOTT: Is this your patch?

RUSSELL: Patch?

TRUSCOTT: Don't you speak English!? Are you local? Christ, there was a time when Hendon ran a course on colloquialisms for officers out of their class. Not any more. Are you local?

WATSON: Just up the road.

TRUSCOTT: You were quick.

WATSON: (*Weakly*) Well, as I said, just up the road.

TRUSCOTT: I thought I was handling this case personally.

RUSSELL: Do you want us to go?

(TRUSCOTT *paces in silence. Something bothers him.*)

TRUSCOTT: Your numbers are the same.

WATSON: Are you a numerologist? Perhaps we were fated to be here.

TRUSCOTT: On the epaulettes . . . the numbers are the same. The Force doesn't usually let officers double up, share an identity. Bad for morale.

WATSON: I lost my tunic and had to borrow one of his to replace it.

TRUSCOTT: What does your station sergeant say about all this?

WATSON: I'm wearing his trousers.

(TRUSCOTT *stops pacing and lights his pipe.*)

TRUSCOTT: Where is the body of the late Mr Halliwell?

RUSSELL: Upstairs.

TRUSCOTT: In Heaven?

RUSSELL: In Miss Milligan's room.

TRUSCOTT: So where's Miss Milligan?

RUSSELL: She's entertaining him with tea and biscuits.

TRUSCOTT: This whole case is very suspicious—a relatively routine call has led me to this nest of vipers.

WATSON: (*Aside to* RUSSELL) Make a note of that Freudian imagery.

TRUSCOTT: Two deaths, one fainting and resurrection, dubious body rubs and now two funny coppers.
(*The slide projector works automatically: slide of* TRUSCOTT *with the library book.*)
All this and blackmail!

RUSSELL: Blackmail?

TRUSCOTT: See here.

RUSSELL: (*Seeing the slide*) It's you.

TRUSCOTT: Brilliant, constable.

WATSON: Okay, then, why have they got a photograph of you?

TRUSCOTT: I arrested them in 1962. The notorious library book boys. Six months apiece and they deserved it.

RUSSELL: Why, what did they do?

TRUSCOTT: You wouldn't have believed it possible. People would be attracted by the lurid covers and then be unfairly disappointed. Dirty words and pictures designed to titillate and shock. It was the complaints from readers who wanted to read smut that alerted me to them.

WATSON: But what did they do?

TRUSCOTT: Defaced library books, you must have heard of them. Front page news in the sensationalist press.
(*Proudly*) My name was mentioned. Looks like I caught up with them again. Couldn't keep their noses out of trouble.
(*Picks up library book.*)
The *Complete Plays* of Christopher Marlowe with some old bugger pasted on the front—this is their kind of artistic style. Pornography! The only question now is who killed them and why?

WATSON: You arrested Joe Orton?

TRUSCOTT: (*Modestly*) Hardly the stature of an Hanratty, for example, but good enough for me.

RUSSELL: (*To* WATSON) I thought you said he was famous.

TRUSCOTT: Hanratty is not without his morbid cult followers—the A6 on a Sunday afternoon is nose-to-tail with them.

WATSON: But Orton's a playwright: he's been on television and radio and chat shows and even *Call My Bluff*.

TRUSCOTT: He was a nobody when I arrested him. Ditto Halliwell. Old matey famous too?

WATSON: No, that was the problem.

TRUSCOTT: What?

RUSSELL: That's why he killed him.

TRUSCOTT: That's why he killed who?

WATSON: That's why Halliwell killed Orton. Or one of the reasons anyway. We didn't know this before we came; we knew he might try to take his life but we knew nothing of Orton's presence and it's only now that we're starting to piece things together.

TRUSCOTT: Is this what they're teaching you at Hendon these days? To talk in riddles? Halliwell killed Orton indeed! They were mates. No, let's tackle the facts . . . death is a great leveller, murder doubly so. Although Halliwell came out of it rather more in one piece than the unfortunate Orton. And no signs of a struggle, which suggests the murderer was known to them.

RUSSELL: Or obsessively tidy, as Halliwell was.

(TRUSCOTT *dips his hand into the pill jar and helps himself to a couple.*)

TRUSCOTT: Want a sweet?

(*They shake their heads.*)

So . . . he came after Orton, found his friend was here and had to get him too to keep him quiet. This slide though . . . it doesn't add up. I feel as if my arrival here has been contrived by person or persons unknown.

Probably the same person or persons who walloped Orton.

WATSON: A trap? There's no cause for paranoia.

TRUSCOTT: Somebody wants me here.

RUSSELL: Revenge?

TRUSCOTT: It's not unheard of. I've sent a lot of villains away, some really hard bastards—split your nostrils as soon as look at you and I wouldn't trust rehabilitation as a cure.

WATSON: It's a bit far-fetched as a scenario.

TRUSCOTT: Defaced library books are a bit far-fetched. A brain over the walls and ceiling is distinctly improbable. Desecrating corpses with tea and biscuits is downright unheard of—a touch of the bloody Aleister Crowley's if you ask me. And who's that Faustus bloke? Where does he fit into all of this?

WATSON: Faustus? *Doctor* Faustus?

TRUSCOTT: I want him found. Their GP, I imagine.

WATSON: *Doctor* Faustus?

TRUSCOTT: Look, all I want is to wrap this case up, put another criminal behind bars and be home in time for tea. If the British Medical Association happen to be involved, we'll nick them too. Get on with it.

WATSON: But Faustus doesn't exist.

TRUSCOTT: Doesn't exist. This is bloody insubordination.

WATSON: But *Doctor Faustus* is the name of a play—I did it at school. Here . . . (*Opens book*) Christopher Marlowe: *Doctor Faustus*.

TRUSCOTT: Then we'll pull Marlowe in. A rival dramatist envious of Orton and his television appearances—it fits!

WATSON: Not really, it doesn't.

TRUSCOTT: Seems pretty watertight to me.

WATSON: Well . . . Marlowe's dead.

TRUSCOTT: Another? This could be a spate of killings. When did this happen?

WATSON: About four hundred years ago.

(TRUSCOTT *calmly lights his pipe.*)

TRUSCOTT: You think you're better than me, I can tell. I've
seen glory boys like you before—cocky bleeders—but
I'll tell you what, my son, I'll break you like I broke
them and I'll tell you something else for free: it'll bloody
hurt. No respect for the dead, just a lust for fame and
attention. You'll stop at nothing to get ahead while the
real law enforcers like me get the dirty work to do. You
can wait your turn on this one, sunshine. I've been
pushed aside once too often to let a young ignoramus
like you steal the limelight. This is my case!
(*The slide projector works automatically:* TRUSCOTT *putting the boot in.*)
What is that man doing?

RUSSELL: The positioning of your regulation footwear
suggests that the man is helping you with your
enquiries.

TRUSCOTT: I believe I am the intended victim of extortion.
This stinks of organized crime, big-league stuff.
(*He quickly checks the body.*)
No sign of knee-capping though. Dead celebrity, candid
photos and a twelve-inch cock in the same room—this is
an Aladdin's cave of gang-land memorabilia.
(*The thought strikes him.*) There's only one bed. Where's
the other bed?

RUSSELL: Other bed?

TRUSCOTT: Someone's nicked the other bed.

WATSON: No.

TRUSCOTT: No? No, what?

WATSON: There wasn't another bed.

TRUSCOTT: What do you mean there wasn't another bed?

RUSSELL: They shared that one.

TRUSCOTT: Shared?

RUSSELL: (*To* WATSON) I thought he knew.

TRUSCOTT: (*Pacing*) We're in bloody trouble here.

RUSSELL: Why trouble, sir?

TRUSCOTT: It's the queer mind. Think what their minds are like when they get up to that with each other. And a pound to a pinch of salt it was another pouf who killed them.
(*The slide changes automatically: the* Entertaining Mr Sloane *reconstruction.*)
WATSON: Inspector.
TRUSCOTT: All of them? Come with me, we haven't a moment to lose.
(*He rushes to the door with* WATSON *and* RUSSELL *in pursuit. They run up the stairs. As they disappear,* SMART *and* GENZIANI *come down the corridor and into the room. They are arguing.*)
SMART: People will be waiting for me. They'll want to know what's happening. I've got my instructions.
GENZIANI: I'll put in a word for you.
SMART: Joe's never late.
GENZIANI: I'm afraid he's going to be eternally late.
SMART: I've got to take him.
GENZIANI: To the meeting? Wouldn't that be rather tasteless?
SMART: It's my job—to collect and deliver.
GENZIANI: I think the demise of your passenger should be taken into account.
SMART: This job's important to me. I don't care how you do it, I was told, just get him there.
GENZIANI: But surely not dead. Your instructions would exclude that.
SMART: I must take him!
(*He gathers up the body of* JOE *and exits.*)
GENZIANI: (*Rushing after him*) Richard, you don't know what you're doing . . .
(*The lights change slightly.* JOE *comes in from the kitchen with a bottle of wine.* KENNETH *is still on the bed.*)
JOE: Did you mean that about you being the inspiration for all of them?
KENNETH: Especially in *Butler*. In this one most of all. It must be subconscious on your part but each of those

characters is me.

JOE: And I was on the verge of saying that I think it's going to be the best thing I've written. Good chance of being Comedy of the Year.

KENNETH: You can still say that, I'll take it as a compliment. Except perhaps the comedy. I don't feel particularly comic.

JOE: (*Word by word*) *What the Butler Saw*. That's a very good title, Kenneth.

KENNETH: What else am I here for other than to inspire? He inspired and expired, his work complete.

JOE: Churchill's cock is starting to be very worrying though. I can see the gleaming knife of censorship being drawn.

KENNETH: I didn't know the Lord Chamberlain practised circumcision.

JOE: Kosher drama! This play is unclean.

KENNETH: Off with its head!
(*They laugh.*)
Write about censorship then.

JOE: In the *Telegraph*? It would be edited out. (*He smirks.*) Why can't people see what I want them to see? Hear what I want them to hear?

KENNETH: Feel what you want them to touch? Because they have to be protected from the likes of you, that's why.

JOE: They know what it's all about. They wouldn't laugh if they didn't.

KENNETH: (*More accurately*) They *couldn't* laugh if they didn't.

JOE: But still we have to live this closeted, claustrophobic life. It makes me sick.

KENNETH: It would decimate the democracy if they found out that most of their household names were corrupt from the arsehole upwards.

JOE: You know what we need? A fully fledged homosexual party in power.

KENNETH: Haven't you heard? We've a queen ruling over us.

JOE: I'd quite like to meet that Black Rod fellow. See if he's all he's cracked up to be.

(KENNETH *drains his glass.*)

You gulped that one down.

KENNETH: I told you, I'm hot.

(KENNETH *turns to the slide projector. He idly flicks through some slides. He comes to the recreation of* Sloane. *He turns away from the slide.*)

JOE: All right?

KENNETH: Me? Same as usual—swings and roundabouts. I might stick to nembutal.

JOE: Brand allegiance, eh? (*Advertising voice*) Nine out of ten paranoid pederasts swear by nembutal!

KENNETH: We do, we do.

(JOE *runs his fingers along the back of* KENNETH's *neck. He looks up to the slide.*)

JOE: Hello, Dicky.

KENNETH: I find him ugly.

JOE: (*Sauntering to the desk*) What do you reckon, then? Go through the plays one by one and chart my development?

KENNETH: Is that according to *Gray's Anatomy* or the drama critic of the *Telegraph*? (*Slight pause*) I can't stand him, you know.

JOE: His views have always been less than flattering.

KENNETH: You know who I'm talking about. Don't you think he's truly ugly?

JOE: (*At desk*) Hmn?

KENNETH: (*Imitating Smart*) Mr Sloane, eh?

(*Gives a very stupid laugh, a low, slow machine gun of a laugh.*)

JOE: (*Trying to ignore*) All right.

KENNETH: Rough trade? He makes Attila the Hun look like Noël Coward.

JOE: Sure.

KENNETH: Ignorant little catamite. One grope and it's eternal devotion.

JOE: Thank you, Kenneth.

KENNETH: And all that leather—he's like an off-cut from a Hell's Angel. And equally oily.

JOE: Is your jealousy going to manifest itself in tired similes?

KENNETH: Me? Jealous of that sponging shit? Give me some credit.

JOE: So I pay? So what? Subsidized sex differs little between Tangiers and Tottenham.

KENNETH: I quite agree . . . but what else are you going to do with your new-found wealth? Spend it on a house in the country?

JOE: I don't want to argue about this, Kenneth. There's no monopoly on my cock.

KENNETH: (*Banging with imaginary gavel*) Sold to the lowest bidder!
(JOE *turns back to his desk and sighs.*)
The open market's never been so open since you joined it. A fact that is transparently obvious to every creep in your circle of friends.

JOE: They're not creeps.

KENNETH: I thought you were the social outsider seeking revenge, the society gatecrasher! No invitation, only a stubborn, barging shoulder. Two years ago you would have had nothing to do with them.

JOE: Move with the times.

KENNETH: Who's that, they ask. Him? That's silly bitch, Halliwell, Joe's scullery maid. Look at the state of him: misery on legs.

JOE: (*Reasonably*) Kenneth.

KENNETH: You can't blame Joe for going on the hunt. You can't though, can you? If that were a house I'd have had it pulled down. Shrieks of camp laughter. The bald-headed fucking nonentity—that's me.

JOE: (*Still calmly*) You were rude to them first with your infantile snobbery.

KENNETH: It was a joke.

47

JOE: You're not a comedian, you never have been. There are codes of conduct.

KENNETH: I don't want to hear about codes of conduct from you of all people.

JOE: It's the only way to make any headway, you know that. I have to infiltrate if I'm going to do anything significant. Attack from the inside.

KENNETH: More vulgar euphemisms?

JOE: What are you winding me up for? Because of a silly photo of a silly boy? You're blowing this out of all proportion again, Kenneth, for Christ's sake. You were all right a minute ago. Where have you put your jar?

KENNETH: And you can stop telling me take tablets to get rid of your headache: it's my head that hurts. Sugar daddy!

JOE: (*Throwing his head back with laughter*) You are jealous. You really are jealous. Possessive idiot.

KENNETH: Bollocks.

JOE: I mean, is that all this is about? A photo? Or is there something else? Some tiny, trivial, insignificant, little thing that has set you screaming. Did I leave footprints, hoofprints, on the linoleum ice-rink? No, no, you forgot the Parmesan and that's my fault too. Fucking hell, Kenneth.

(*Pause.* JOE *goes to his desk.*)

KENNETH: Will you answer me one question?

JOE: If that's the question—yes.

(*No response.*)

You and your questions, you could have been the Michael Miles of the Gestapo. You have one minute to tell me ze plans of ze bomb factory vizout ze jawohl or ze nein answers, starting from now.

KENNETH: I have one question.

JOE: And tonight's star prize is a very hot shower!

KENNETH: Will you answer my question?

JOE: (*Ordering*) Open ze box. (*Even more harshly*) Take ze money!

KENNETH: Will you answer my question?

JOE: Can anyone enjoy arguing this much?

KENNETH: Will you answer my question?

JOE: No.

KENNETH: Why not?

JOE: I can see the tripwire, Kenneth, as the searchlight swings round. Yes, it's a lovely, tempting bit of open ground but halfway across I'd hit that wire and get raked by machine-gun fire. So sorry, but no.
(*Pause.*)

KENNETH: Will you answer my question?
(*Pause.*)

JOE: What is it this time?

KENNETH: When did you decide to leave me?

JOE: I've heard it before.

KENNETH: Then you should know the answer.

JOE: I haven't decided to leave you, Kenneth.

KENNETH: But you want to.

JOE: I do not want to.

KENNETH: I know you do.

JOE: (*Exasperated*) Oh Kenneth . . .

KENNETH: Don't you?

JOE: I don't know what the hell to say to satisfy you.

KENNETH: Don't say anything.

JOE: All right, I won't say anything.

KENNETH: Sixteen years! Sixteen years and now this!

JOE: Yeah, well, sheer bliss isn't everything, Kenneth.

KENNETH: I've tolerated sometimes even envied your dalliances. I've watched you take the applause. I've sat here on my own whilst you have an apparently exclusive business meeting which only turns out to be the biggest fucking social gathering of the year and never—never!— have you turned round and said, 'Well, actually, I owe a great deal to my lover and mentor, Kenneth Halliwell.'

JOE: You have not written my plays, Kenneth. Any similarity between characters living or dead is purely of your own wish-fulfilment. They're characters in plays, they're not you. It's the same old argument again. Snakes and bloody ladders, night after night. Up one, down the other—up and down, up and down, like a wanker on a trampoline.

KENNETH: Sixteen years is a long time for my creativity to play second fiddle. I could have done something with myself, made a name for myself.

JOE: Yes, Kenneth, I suppose you could. (*Mocking*) And this is the gratitude you receive.

KENNETH: I hate you. You're a smug, self-obsessed imposter. When I lifted you from the gutter you were nothing. A typist! You couldn't act and the only writing you did was in that adolescent diary . . .

JOE: But you nurtured me until I blossomed.

KENNETH: A cuckoo in my nest.

JOE: Do shut up.

KENNETH: That wonderful brain of yours was nothing—a dirty waiting-room for dreams. I didn't know then that your dreams meant the end of mine.

JOE: What do you want from me? What could satisfy you? A marriage certificate that says that although we are both bent as corkscrews we're happily married and don't have compatibility problems?

KENNETH: Fuck off, you ponce.

JOE: Such eloquence. Yes, I know we're both a wee bit strange but we are hoping to raise a family in the near future. Kenneth can't have babies, according to our gynaecologist, but God, they tell us, knows best, so what we've thought of doing is importing a dozen Moroccan boys to attend us in our old age. Or rather in my old age because Kenneth's somewhat antique already . . .

KENNETH: You clever bastard!

(*He swings at* JOE *with all his strength and catches him just above the ear.* JOE *stares at him in anger and resentment, fuming. He might retaliate, it seems. After some moments, and just in*

50

control, he turns and storms to the kitchen. KENNETH *is left there, also fuming. The door behind him bursts open and* TRUSCOTT *rushes in.*)

TRUSCOTT: You'd better leave Mr Orton alone!
(*They stand face to face.*)

BLACKOUT

ACT TWO

A phone is ringing.

The lights rise on the downstairs flat. KENNETH *is sitting on the end of the bed, disturbed.*

JOE *enters to answer the phone.*

KENNETH: I'm sorry, Joe. Joe, I'm sorry, I got upset and I didn't know what I was doing. I can't help myself, Joe, believe me.

JOE: Shut up, Kenneth. Take some tablets. Preferably one too many.

(*Answers phone.*)

Hello? Yes, this is Joe . . . Roger . . . you still want to see that film. (*Pause*) No, I'd rather not. Not tonight. I'm on the wrong end of the slings and arrows. (*Pause*) Yes, that's right. 'The Life and Times of Joe Orton'. Read all about me on Sunday morning. That should put you off Rice Crispies. (*Chuckle*) And don't I know it! Look, I really can't talk at the moment. (*Pause*) Okay then. When better? (*Slight pause*) If I'm not here Clytemnestra will take a message. (*Pause*) If you like. Lunchtime? Right. Take care, Roger. Goodnight. And you!

(*Replaces receiver.*)

Satisfied?

KENNETH: (*Feebly*) Joe.

JOE: I have a vision of Hell. There is a long, long line of Kenneth Halliwells stretching into the hot infinity. The noise is almost unbearable: wailing, howling, shouting and screaming and for some reason, some deep, inexplicable reason, I have to try to calm them all down. Why it is down to me I don't know but I have to do it. One by one I have to plead with them and pacify them. One by one. And they hit and scratch and fight. And there are hundreds of millions of them. And I used to love every one.

(*Silence.*)

Maybe I should move out, Kenneth.

(*The lights fade on them and rise on* GENZIANI's *flat.* SMART *is tied to a chair.* TRUSCOTT *and* GENZIANI *stand.*)

TRUSCOTT: Twenty-five years I've spent defending this country from all manner of assaults and never yet have I encountered such a gross compendium of immorality.

SMART: You ought to get out more. Join the army and see the world.

TRUSCOTT: I'll have less of your lip. I've served my Queen and Country which is more than could be said for you. Your entire view of the world has been framed by the rear window of cars.

SMART: I've a pretty good idea of what life must look like bent double in khaki—it's all the same in the services.

GENZIANI: Richard!

TRUSCOTT: You'd have been one of the first to get a dishonourable discharge. You listen to me—there are no poufs in the services.

SMART: That's not what one of my uncles told me.

TRUSCOTT: He'll be talking of wartime then: that's camaraderie—a mutual intimacy, social, you know. I'll agree that in times of stress some of the lads would help each other out, but they're great big blokes with muscles like footballs. You couldn't call them homosexuals . . . they'd belt you one.

SMART: A spade's a spade.

TRUSCOTT: You've heard of the Dunkirk Spirit? That's what Churchill was referring to: this special *esprit de corps* and the need to all pull together. All those blokes are married now with wives and kiddies—see what happens when the civilians try it though . . . blood all over the show.

53

These pansies going on their marches is all wrong. Hundreds of them, mincing through the streets, brazen as you please—drop a ten-bob note and you daren't pick it up. And all that bloody perfume! The scent of a decaying civilization, I call it . . .

GENZIANI: I wonder if Mr Smart may be released. The rope is cutting into his skin.

TRUSCOTT: There may well be biblical precedent for body-snatching but that was of a Messiah and in a foreign country too. British law cannot condone such an act.

GENZIANI: If the boy says he needs the corpse, he obviously must need a corpse. People don't ask for such things for purely gratuitous reasons. Unless of course they were spoilt as a child. And then only if a friend had one.

TRUSCOTT: Very broadminded, Mr Genziani.

GENZIANI: For the sake of a carcass it seems foolish for the boy to lose his job.

(*The lights fade on them and rise on the flat below.* JOE *at his desk;* KENNETH *sitting on the bed.*)

JOE: (*Making notes*) *Entertaining Mr Sloane.* The breakthrough to the stage. Set the trend for future work. Notion of covert sexuality and maintenance of appearances.

(*He seems unhappy with this.*)

The struggle for dominance . . .

(*He screws the paper into a ball.*)

Fuck it.

(*Pause.*)

KENNETH: Are you going to the studios in the morning?

(JOE *doesn't answer.*)

Young Richard will be picking you up, though, won't he?

JOE: He is a chauffeur. Picking up is all in a day's work.

KENNETH: What time can I expect you home?

JOE: I don't know, it's a stupid question. I'll be home when it's finished. Unless I decide to go for a drink or something.

KENNETH: Promise me you won't just walk away.

JOE: (*Turning it into a ballad*) Promise me you won't just walk away. Promise me you'll stay . . . don't be so melodramatic. (*Slight pause*) We're different now, Kenneth, mutually incompatible. We've never been this bad before. A lot has changed.

KENNETH: Water under the bridge of thighs.

JOE: Don't go tart on me.

KENNETH: You obviously have something to say—speak that which has to be spoken.

JOE: I thought you wanted an answer to your question.

KENNETH: No.

JOE: Forget it, then. I only had excuses anyway.

KENNETH: You didn't even have them.

(*The phone rings.* KENNETH *snaps.*)

Are we living in a fucking telephone exchange?

(*Answers, a sweet voice through clenched teeth*) Good evening, the residence of Joe Orton, playwright and *bon viveur* . . . (*His face relaxes suddenly and his voice loses its anger.*)

. . . Oh, doctor, yes, it is Kenneth, how on earth did you guess? (*Pause*) Of course I'm fine. I thought it was someone for Joe. It was only a joke. (*Covers receiver*) You humourless bastard. (*Opens again*) Yes, I am taking the tablets and they're just what you ordered. (*A lame laugh*) No, I won't be going out. Joe? Are you going out this evening, Joe?

(JOE *turns away.*)

He's refusing to commit himself. (*Pointedly*) Unlike some of us. (*Pause. His face displays a new seriousness.*) What time tomorrow? (*Pause*) Yes, I'll be here. Thank you for calling, doctor. Goodnight.

(*He replaces the receiver.*)

JOE: What was all that about?

KENNETH: He wanted to know how I feel.

JOE: Did you get him to phone?

KENNETH: Don't be stupid.

55

JOE: You really are sick, aren't you, Kenneth?

KENNETH: Was that a rhetorical question?

JOE: Was that?

(JOE *has been using the projector during the phone call. Slide:* JOE *and* KENNETH *with tourists, in Morocco.*)

KENNETH: (*Smoking and looking at slide*) Friends in faraway places. A conversation about semen on leopard-skin carpets for the mortification of tourists. Playing to the audience. Gratuitous smut. (*Pause*) I think one of us must be.

(*The lights fade on them and rise on* MISS MILLIGAN's *room.* WATSON *and* RUSSELL *in earnest discussion. The bodies are reunited, propped up in chairs.* MISS MILLIGAN *is still talking to the body of* KENNETH.)

RUSSELL: You think she'd let the poor bloke enjoy his eternal slumber. She hasn't let him get a word in edgeways for over an hour. Not that he could if she did.

WATSON: (*Troubled*) Shut up. This thesis is floundering.

RUSSELL: It had to, didn't it. The minute we got here I knew we were stuffed but, no, we had to carry on to satisfy you. The thirst for knowledge.

WATSON: Look, if it hadn't been for you forcing me to read all those books I'd never have got into psychology. You're as much to blame as me.

RUSSELL: You dragged me here.

WATSON: It's so frustrating—there he is, the neurotic classic, and he can't answer even the most innocent of questions.

RUSSELL: We killed him.

WATSON: Don't let Truscott hear you say that.

RUSSELL: If he hadn't known we were coming, none of this would have happened.

WATSON: How can you say that? We did everything in our powers to allay his fears—we even dressed up as policemen to ask 'a few routine questions, sir. If we

mentioned the colour green, what would be the first
thing that comes into your head?'

RUSSELL: The perfect guise for a cross examination, you said.
Great thinking, Batman.

WATSON: It could have worked.

RUSSELL: Sure. It would have been as successful as dressing
up as Peter Pan and Tinkerbell and gatecrashing a
rugby club dinner. And don't analyse that imagery.

WATSON: I wasn't going to. We'll have to try a different
tack. . . .

(*Lights fade on them and rise on* GENZIANI's *room.* SMART *is
still trussed to the chair.*)

TRUSCOTT: So what about that slide?

SMART: It was a joke.

TRUSCOTT: (*Dryly*) Ha ha ha.

SMART: It amused Joe.

TRUSCOTT: Joe?

GENZIANI: The late Mr Orton.

TRUSCOTT: All right. First-name terms was it?

SMART: Everyone called him Joe.

TRUSCOTT: Very progressive of him, breaking down the class
barriers. (*Menacing*) Where's the joke?

GENZIANI: The joke is that Joe—Mr Orton—was frequently
amused by the way he saw real life mirroring his art.
And this slide you refer to was a mock cast photograph,
if you like, of 'Entertaining Mr Sloane', his first stage
play. I wasn't deeply impressed with either the play or
the fact that I resembled one of the characters but I am
prepared to make concessions for other people's
enjoyment.

TRUSCOTT: So you, you and the woman are reflections of his
twisted imagination. Very comical. I imagine Joe has
taken his sense of humour to the grave with him.

(*As he passes* SMART *he catches a scent.*)

Perfume?

SMART: It's special stuff for my knotted muscles.

(TRUSCOTT *looks sceptical and continues pacing*.)

TRUSCOTT: You knew Orton rather well. You came here this morning to take him to the film studios. You knocked on the door, received no answer and in a fit of anger you killed these people.

SMART: What?

TRUSCOTT: Don't substitute the word 'what' for 'yes'.

SMART: What?

TRUSCOTT: You no longer realize what you're saying. Unless you're trying to bluff your way into a plea of diminished responsibility. Well, it won't work.

GENZIANI: You talk as if the boy did it.

TRUSCOTT: A case like this, it's the guilty who have to prove their innocence.

SMART: I'm not guilty of nothing.

TRUSCOTT: Your car down there?

SMART: Yeah.

TRUSCOTT: (*Finishing the sentence*) On the double yellow lines? See? There's one crime unwittingly committed. Who's to say you haven't murdered these men? Easily done, quick bash with a heavy-duty prick, a slip of the hand. Why did you murder them?

SMART: I didn't murder them.

TRUSCOTT: Then why deny it?

(*The lights fade on them and rise on the downstairs flat.* JOE *and* KENNETH *as before*.)

KENNETH: I think I shall phone the physician.

JOE: (*Looking up from the desk*) What the hell for? You've only just spoken to him.

KENNETH: No, Joe, I've just spoken to you, now I'm going to speak to my doctor.

(*Dials seven digits and spells out a letter with each*.)

S . . . H . . . I . . . T . . . B . . . A . . . G . . . shitbag!

(*He is cheerful, a forced gaiety*.)

Shitbag.

(*The act is wearing thin and he needs the doctor to answer*.)

Come on . . . come on . . .

(*Suddenly*) Doctor? Kenneth Halliwell again. I'm calling to confirm our somewhat recent conversation.

(*He looks straight into* JOE.)

About my hospitalization. And, yes, I will be in tomorrow morning to talk to the psychiatrists. No question of missing that. Joe's going to be out but I'll certainly be here.

(*Pause. This is for* JOE*'s benefit.*)

And I'm perfectly all right at the moment, yes. A few tempests in teacups, but otherwise I'm a mental Rock of Gibraltar. So that's inked in now, is it? Good. Well, that's all I wanted to talk about, I'll let you get back to real life now. Thank you for your patience with a patient. Goodnight.

(*He replaces the receiver very delicately.*)

JOE: (*After a short 'disinterested' pause*) Will a psychiatrist help?

KENNETH: I very much doubt it—that's why he's sending two.

JOE: Would anything help?

KENNETH: Recognition. Acknowledgement. A listener?

JOE: *The Boy Hairdresser?*

KENNETH: Or my other unpublished works of dementia? Neatly typed, gathering dust and going yellow? What does that remind me of? Oh yes, that's right, it reminds me of *me*.

JOE: Submit something else.

KENNETH: What's the point? They've been rejected hundreds of times before, only now they'll think I'm trying to cash in on you.

JOE: They wouldn't link you with me.

KENNETH: (*Bitterly*) No, you're probably right.

JOE: You don't give me a chance—don't patronize me, I don't need your sympathy, I'm better off on my own . . . You're the drowning man who only waves manuscripts.

KENNETH: All right, all right, the psychiatrists it is!

59

JOE: (*Not following*) What?

KENNETH: I'll be certified as insane if I'm lucky: 'I'm sorry,
     Mr Halliwell, but we have to inform you that you have
     lived your entire life under a gross misapprehension.'

JOE: Leave it, Kenneth.

KENNETH: 'It is the homosexual side of you as we see things.
     Deep down, Mr Halliwell, you hate homosexuals—in
     fact this is the first case of terminal homosexuality we've
     encountered. It is a clinical certainty that man was
     never intended to conjugate with man and this is why
     there are women. We may be a bit late to stop the rot
     but repeat after us: Homosexuals are a pain in the arse;
     homosexuals are a pain in the arse. I hate homosexuals.
     I hate Joe stinking Orton!'
     (*The lights fade on them and rise on* GENZIANI's *room. The
     interrogation continues.*)

TRUSCOTT: Untie the young man would you, sir?
     (GENZIANI *does so.*)

GENZIANI: Isn't this rather unorthodox for a policeman?

TRUSCOTT: We're not all Dixons of Dock Green smiling for
     the camera—someone's got to fight the real crime.
     Depends what you want the police for: to tell the time
     or to keep criminals at bay? I'd happily spend all day
     flexing my calves and smiling at foreigners, but in that
     time three banks will have been robbed, two women will
     have been raped and your house will have been burned
     to the ground by a frenzied arsonist. Would you drop
     this for me please?
     (*Hands him a banknote.*)

GENZIANI: What is it?

TRUSCOTT: A ten-shilling note. You've seen one before.

GENZIANI: (*Puzzled*) And you want me to drop it?
     (TRUSCOTT *indicates that he does.*)
     What? Anywhere?
     (TRUSCOTT *indicates to drop it in front of* SMART. GENZIANI
     does so.)

And now?

TRUSCOTT: I'd like you to pick it up for me if you'd be so
kind.

(GENZIANI, *his puzzlement clear, does so.*)

GENZIANI: (*Handing it to him*) There you are.

TRUSCOTT: Well, Mr Smart?

SMART: Yeah?

TRUSCOTT: Did I not detect a slight tremor ripple through
your loins?

SMART: I'm still trying to get my blood circulating after being
tied up like a chicken.

TRUSCOTT: You don't give anything away, do you?

SMART: Not on my salary.

TRUSCOTT: And what is your salary?

SMART: Average.

TRUSCOTT: Only average? Twenty-guinea shoes, solid gold
bracelet, expensive Swiss watch and flash leather wear?
You're better dressed than my Chief Superintendent.

SMART: The perks.

TRUSCOTT: He gets his fair share.

SMART: I drive for rich people who tip well.

TRUSCOTT: People like Orton?

SMART: Yeah.

TRUSCOTT: (*Chewing his pipe*) The bodies and the blood apart,
which would cheapen any room, was that the flat of a
very rich man? No, it wasn't. So what you are talking,
Mr Smart, is the biggest load of bollocks this side of
Christmas.

SMART: I can't help where Joe lived.

TRUSCOTT: And died.

SMART: Maybe he wanted to move out.

TRUSCOTT: You've reduced your statement to a shambles.

GENZIANI: Surely this is no more than routine questioning,
Inspector. Richard has made no statement and you've
written nothing down.

TRUSCOTT: I don't have to. If I need it, I can always write it

61

out later and get him to sign it. It saves an awful
lot of paper work.

GENZIANI: But you can't do that.

TRUSCOTT: I assure you I can—believe me, I make most of
my convictions in this way.

GENZIANI: That's disgraceful.

TRUSCOTT: I lure the suspect into a false sense of security
without my notebook, they blabber on and on and —
wham!—I've got them by their unlawful short and
curlies.

SMART: You bastard.

TRUSCOTT: You'd have to talk to my mother about that.
(*Changes tack smoothly*) It doesn't matter to me if your
sexual bread is buttered on the other side as it were, Mr
Smart. The law is changing, attitudes are changing and
I like to keep abreast of the trends. Is the grass greener
on the other side of the hill?

SMART: What if I said it was?

TRUSCOTT: I'd beat the living shit out of you.
(*The lights fade on them and rise on* MISS MILLIGAN's *room.*
MISS MILLIGAN *is STILL talking.* RUSSELL *and* WATSON *are*
taking stock of the situation. The bodies sit.)

MILLIGAN: So I said to her, this is the woman with the
bunion remember, that if that's their attitude they can
keep their rotten buses—I'll walk. Not that she could,
the poor woman, not with that bunion.

WATSON: The woman's speech is peppered with red things
longer than they're wide—buses, cars, ice lollies,
post-boxes. I wonder if she knows exactly how much of
her personality she's flaunting when she posts a letter.

RUSSELL: I'm not interested anymore. We've been swept
along too far, we're out of our depths. You may be in
your element but I'm certainly not. The whole thing has
passed the point of fun. May I remind you of the
Pleasure Principle?

WATSON: (*Ignoring him*) Miss Milligan, if I may break off your

62

intercourse with the other world for a moment . . .
how long had Mr Halliwell borne a grudge against Mr
Orton?

MILLIGAN: Oooh . . . let me think . . . I really wouldn't like to
say. They've been at it like knives for years.

WATSON: At what??

RUSSELL: I often think that's the only reason you followed me
into psychology—so you could listen to dirty stories.

MILLIGAN: I think it was the diary as much as anything.

WATSON: Diary? What diary?

MILLIGAN: Joe's diary. It was absolutely shocking.

RUSSELL: You saw the diary.

WATSON: No I didn't.

RUSSELL: Lying beside Halliwell. With the note. If you read
the diary all will be explained.

WATSON: No.

RUSSELL: I thought you'd deliberately ignored it.

WATSON: Everyone was getting hysterical. All I saw was the
whites of people's eyes.

RUSSELL: It must still be downstairs.

WATSON: Did Truscott see it?

RUSSELL: He saw the note. He threw the diary away.

WATSON: What are we waiting for? This is the piece in the
jigsaw we've been missing.

RUSSELL: We're meant to be guarding the bodies.

WATSON: To hell with the bodies. Miss Milligan?

MILLIGAN: Yes, dear?

WATSON: They're not to leave the room.

MILLIGAN: Shall I make another pot?

WATSON: They'd like that. (*To* RUSSELL) Come on.

(*The lights fade on them and rise on the downstairs flat.* JOE *at
the desk.* KENNETH *standing idly by.*)

JOE: Kenneth, will you stop loitering about? What are you
waiting for? A bit of my genius to fall into your hands?

KENNETH: I'm not that patient.

(JOE *tries to ignore him.*)

Am I disturbing you?

(JOE's *glare makes him drift away—not too hurriedly—to the slide projector. He flicks through a few. He comes to the one of the* Evening Standard *Drama Awards.*)

Look, Joe, the invitation for your woman to attend the awards. Mrs Orton! If they'd seen the stretch marks I've seen. I should have dressed up, of course, but I only have these rags.

JOE: Your off-the-peg sackcloth and ashes.

KENNETH: I sat here, I remember, scrubbing the lino waiting for an hirsute fairy with a bass voice to come and whisk me away—You shall go to the *Evening Standard* Drama Awards, my dear, you shall.

JOE: If you're fed up with me why don't you go back to kissing frogs?

KENNETH: I kissed one once and my hair fell out.

JOE: My fault again.

KENNETH: (*Innocently*) I'm trying to collect material for your piece.

JOE: For which I'm very grateful but no one would want to hear about your self-pity.

KENNETH: The psychiatrist would.

JOE: I know he would: he gets paid for it.

KENNETH: (*Sweetly*) And what do you get paid for, Joe?

JOE: Not for sitting here all night getting my head chewed off. Christ, Kenneth, you're like bloody Scheherazade with your endless round of stories.

KENNETH: I'm not keeping you up, am I?

JOE: Or rather: Aesop with his fucking fables—every one a moral chestnut. I don't like morals from you, Kenneth. You couldn't set an example if your life depended on it.

KENNETH: Not that it would really matter to anyone if it did.

(JOE *turns his back to* KENNETH *again—disgusted and annoyed.* KENNETH *finds some slides in the box and deliberately flicks one at the back of* JOE's *head.* JOE *doesn't look round but uses the tired voice . . .*)

JOE: Fuck off, Kenneth.
> (KENNETH *flicks another slide.* JOE *ignores it.* KENNETH *flicks a third.*)
> (*Swinging round, angrily*) These pathetic taunts with our past. Happy memories?
> (*He twists the slide in his fingers and breaks it.*)

KENNETH: (*Pouts*) I do believe we're losing our temper.
> (JOE *turns back to the desk, sullen.* KENNETH *waits for him to resume his work and then archly flicks a fourth slide.* JOE *turns—livid.*)

JOE: You wonder why I want to leave? You're intolerable.

KENNETH: Sixteen short years . . .

JOE: It hasn't all been like this.

KENNETH: It has for me.

JOE: I can't work now without you jumping about, flinging your disintegrating ego across the desk . . .

KENNETH: You're tearing me apart with your cold-heartedness. I'm bleeding to death in front of you, and all you worry about are your fucking manuscripts!

JOE: I'm not going to sacrifice myself on your altar, Kenneth, fifteen years or not. You insult my friends, you argue at nothing, you kill me socially—I can't cope with your life and you can't cope with mine. You fuss about, preening and cleaning, but I'm living on your nerves and that simply won't do. Okay, then, what if we did get a bigger place—a house—like that one in Brighton. What then? Would your problems dissolve? No . . .

KENNETH: Bugger Bognor—fuck Brighton! You'd have your prick parties for the sycophantic pall-bearers of your leaden wit and I'd be stuffed into the kitchen with my neuroses. A bucket of tranquillizers to bobble me along to the next torture with the psychiatrist and his deeply meaningful questions about my pathetic existence from afterbirth to afterlife. Your mother? Died from a wasp sting? An unusual mode of mortality but indisputably tragic. And your father, how did he shuffle off this

mortal coil? Put his head in a gas stove. That's more
like it! A decidedly more conventional solution to the
problem posed by life but an undeniable contribution
to your unhappy childhood. Unhappy, doctor? On
the contrary, schooldays were the happiest days of
my life.

(*His head drops. He is silent.*)

Help me, Joe.

JOE: I'll get you a cocoa.

(*After a brief moment of indecision he goes to the kitchen. The
front door opens slowly.* WATSON *and* RUSSELL's *heads appear.*
KENNETH *looks up in fear. The lights fade on them and rise on*
GENZIANI's *room.* GENZIANI, TRUSCOTT *and* SMART *as before.*)

GENZIANI: I really must protest, this is quite scandalous. I
will not see this young man subjected to these
degradations.

TRUSCOTT: He's a murderer.

GENZIANI: Twaddle. Even if he were this is no way to treat
him.

TRUSCOTT: Oh my Christ, a liberal. 'Don't gaol them, give
them another chance, they didn't mean to do it.' You
make me sick with your dung-spinning soft options.
Civil liberties? Balls! The man's a killer. A homo killing
other homos. Mind you, that's not a bad thing: at this
rate two-thirds of them'll be in their graves and the
other third will be locked up.

GENZIANI: Making the streets fit for clean and decent people.

TRUSCOTT: You're not a nance as well?

GENZIANI: No, I try to understand.

TRUSCOTT: Read a book on it, have you? Consenting adults.
Who the hell would consent to that? No one in their
right bloody minds.

GENZIANI: You are a very narrow-minded man.

TRUSCOTT: I simply represent the law, Mr Genziani.

GENZIANI: But surely homosexuality is no longer a crime!

TRUSCOTT: Neither's Nazism, my liberal friend, but you may

look on me as the Met's equivalent of Simon Wiesenthal.

GENZIANI: Do you have any credentials?

(TRUSCOTT *hands him an ID card*)

Since when has the Metropolitan Water Board been able to persecute people in their own homes?

TRUSCOTT: (*Snatching it back and handing another*) Purely for undercover work. The MWB is very helpful. We will locate missing water mains for them and they, in turn, will refer saturated corpses to us. The way people flout authority these days we have to stick together if we are to get any work done. Satisfied?

GENZIANI: Unfortunately, yes.

TRUSCOTT: If it weren't for his confession, he'd probably be on his way by now. It's the homosexuality, you see. Prosecution will emphasize the frenzied nature of the attack and then push the psychopathic homosexual bit—you have to be mad to be queer and so forth . . . they'll convict.

GENZIANI: That is a very bigoted attitude, Inspector.

TRUSCOTT: What they all need is a good talking to over a crème de menthe and a length of hosepipe.

GENZIANI: I can't agree with you, I'm afraid.

TRUSCOTT: (*Picking up on this*) Afraid? What is there to be frightened of, Mr *Genziani*?

(*He rolls the name across his tongue.*)

GENZIANI: I didn't mean I was frightened.

TRUSCOTT: Then perhaps you should be. Life can be very unpredictable. Why, at any moment, a phallus-wielding turd burglar could burst through that door and smash your face in. Or you could suddenly be arrested for the murder of a famous playwright.

GENZIANI: Are you threatening me?

TRUSCOTT: It's a fine Italian name . . . Genziani.

GENZIANI: My father was from Florence.

TRUSCOTT: (*Beginning to probe*) You'll be familiar with the dishes of your paternal country then.

GENZIANI: Yes.

TRUSCOTT: Spaghetti bolognese?

GENZIANI: (*Suspicious*) Yes.

TRUSCOTT: (*Allaying suspicions*) A very nice dish.
(*The lights fade on them and rise on the downstairs flat.
RUSSELL and WATSON are facing KENNETH.*)

WATSON: Well, well, well.

RUSSELL: Well, well, well.

WATSON: Well. This must be rather disturbing for you, Mr
Halliwell. Kenneth. (*He smiles.*) It's not every day this
happens, eh?

RUSSELL: Not even in your average blue moon.

WATSON: You're obviously a very sick man indeed. You
see . . . you're not sure that we're here and, I think I
speak for both of us, we're not sure that you're here. We
left your rather lifeless . . .

RUSSELL: Definitely lifeless.

WATSON: . . . form upstairs. (*Doctor voice*) I hope this isn't too
harrowing.

RUSSELL: (*Trying to cheer him up*) I'll be honest, it's scaring the
crap out of me.

WATSON: The problem as I see it, is this, Kenneth. You're
dead. Somewhat stone cold, I know I'm being morbid
but I don't see any other way round it. You know that
you've killed Mr Orton.

RUSSELL: Or that you're going to kill Mr Orton.

WATSON: It's the only way.

RUSSELL: There's a hell of a furore about it all.
(*KENNETH grabs some tablets and gulps them down.*)
Now they won't help, will they. Really, Mr Halliwell.
(*KENNETH closes his eyes.*)
You'll have to face the facts, I'm afraid.
(*Taps him on the shoulder.*)
Hello!

WATSON: Come on, get a grip on yourself. You're not shrink-resistant. Open your eyes, we're still here. There's just one question that's been bothering us. Why?

RUSSELL: Yes, why kill Mr Orton as well as yourself. I mean, your suicide has been inevitable for some time but no one spotted the murder.

WATSON: And that's interesting. If we could just have your answer we'll be on our way.

RUSSELL: We came down for the diary. Is it the diary? Will we find the answer in the diary?

WATSON: (*To* RUSSELL) We will. So what is it then, Mr Halliwell? Envy?

RUSSELL: Wasted life?

WATSON: Frustrated ambition?

RUSSELL: Unrequited love?

WATSON: Bad sex?

RUSSELL: That was a bit unfair.

WATSON: Exclusion?

RUSSELL: Isolation?

KENNETH: (*Nearly screaming*) Get out!

(*The lights fade on them and rise on* MISS MILLIGAN's *room. This is real time in the evening.* MISS MILLIGAN *is dressed for bed. Elegant perhaps in contrast to her appearance so far in the action.*)

MILLIGAN: There's no need to shout, Kenneth.

(*The lights fade on her and rise on* GENZIANI's *room. Similarly,* GENZIANI *is now on his own. He is relaxing with a drink. He wears a dressing-gown or similar. He shakes his head at the shout.*)

GENZIANI: Arguing again?

(*The lights fade on him and rise on the downstairs flat.* RUSSELL *and* WATSON *have disappeared.* JOE *bursts in.*)

JOE: What the hell is wrong?

KENNETH: Leave me alone!

BLACKOUT

ACT THREE

The sound of typing.
  The lights rise on the downstairs flat.
  JOE *is working at the desk—the typewriter.* KENNETH, *his cocoa finished beside him, sits reading his library book.*

KENNETH: Now, Dido, with these relics burn thyself. And make Aeneas famous through the world for perjury and slaughter of a queen.

JOE: (*Typing*) Dido, Queen of Carthage—Kenneth, Queen of Islington.
  (*Pause. The sound of typing.*)

KENNETH: An evening of battle-weary incommunicado, is it?

JOE: You're better then. It's late, I'm not trying any more.

KENNETH: Exactly what were you attempting?
  (JOE *ignores him.*)
  New-found reticence? What a day for discoveries this has turned out to be.

JOE: Don't push your luck again, Kenneth.

KENNETH: Am I too emotional for you?
  (JOE *ignores this.*)
  I wonder if it's because I have a heart?

JOE: I don't?

KENNETH: Of course you do, Joe. In your scrotum.

JOE: What I have in my scrotum is the answer to all your taunts: bollocks! (*Sarcastic*) I am the physical person. I enjoy being physical. I can only relate to people when they're wriggling beneath me. Me Tarzan—you Jane.

KENNETH: I wouldn't beat your chest—you might set up waves of vibrations through the fat and unsettle your brain.

JOE: Sensitivity is a word I associate with the condom.

KENNETH: More epigrammatic crap.

70

JOE: So where have your feelings got you? Stop taking those chemicals and you're bent double with guilt pains. Your whole life has been spent balancing uppers with downers without ever finding the happy mean. Me? Nasty, physical, FUNDAMENTAL me—I don't give a toss in a solid gold bucket for you chain-smoking, emotional acrobats. I can release all of my foibles and anxieties in one sexually promiscuous act with another living creature. The energy I lose is replaced by an energy I use.

KENNETH: (*Ignoring this and seizing diary*) *The Diary of a Somebody*.

JOE: Yet another good title.

KENNETH: It's the story of my life, I don't know why you put your name on the front. I might copy it out and rename it—how about *Kenneth Halliwell: Usage and Abusage*?

JOE: I don't make you read it.

KENNETH: Oh, but I like to—all that bitchiness, the snide footnotes . . .

JOE: In future I shall leave a space for you to enter your thoughts below mine. If we have a future.

KENNETH: This is the testament to everything that's wrong with you. Look in here and you'll find that you've lived out every play you've ever written—it's happened to you, it's happened to me, it's happened to us.

JOE: What an exciting life we lead.

KENNETH: Only you're such a thug you don't realize.

JOE: I've realized my life, Kenneth, which is more than you could ever hope to do.

KENNETH: Animal! Rut your way to fame and fortune!

JOE: How true.

KENNETH: Get rid of your taboos by shoving them up your victim. Put them on stage and have your sins absolved by laughter.

JOE: Bless me, Father.

KENNETH: Joe Orton: a play, a smile, a Kleenex.

71

JOE: Do shut up, for fuck's sake.

KENNETH: No.

(*Pause*)

Did you answer my question?

JOE: I've weighed up the pros and cons.

KENNETH: Have you? Can you? For the first time in your baby-oiled life you're being threatened by someone being close to you. No one's ever been this close to you—not your mother, not your father . . . the hunter has be ome the hunted.

JOE: Hunted? Who's hunting me? It's certainly not you. You're not a predator, you're a parasite. I'm going to get my independence.

KENNETH: The voice of America and look what happened there—messy, very messy.

JOE: Don't you threaten me, Kenneth. You're no longer the red light of my life.

KENNETH: You've left it a bit late to be footloose and fancy-free, I'd have thought. At long last the success you've always dreamed of, and you're too old to savour its juices. You're the wrong side of thirty, babe. You've only little Moroccan boys left now. It's going to be torture.

JOE: At least I won't be stuck in this Chamber of Horrors.

KENNETH: Then you'll realize.

JOE: (*Mocking*) I gave you the best years of my life.

KENNETH: You noticed, did you?

JOE: The man with the Midas touch. You turned me to gold—

KENNETH: Fool's gold.

JOE: . . . and yourself to wood so that you could make more crosses to bear.

KENNETH: I'm glad you're going.

JOE: You're letting me go? I thought I'd need written permission.

KENNETH: Your diary gave you that a long time ago. I'm

surprised by your endurance under the
circumstances. It must have been pretty hellish.

JOE: I like having things done for me.

KENNETH: Only that reason?

JOE: Well, Kenneth, as I have no emotions it couldn't be
anything else keeping me here. But now your term of
utility has expired and you have become excessively
dependent on my presence. As a servant you have been
adequate, if a little presumptuous—as a human being
your performance has been ill-conceived and
inconsistent. You're not even particularly good in
support.

KENNETH: (*Ending the review*) Twat-brain: the *Sunday
Telegraph*.

JOE: In the comedy of my life the last thing I need is a
straight man. You'll be an unwanted old queen who
fusses over the housework from dawn till dusk and who
has to take ten valium to cope with the excitement of
paying the milkman.

KENNETH: While you troll around until no one wants a
lubricated old playwright any more. Then you'll sit
outside primary schools on games days and leer at little
boys in their white, starched shorts. And you'll grunt
and you'll mumble and you'll wank in your pants . . .
maybe I will be lonely but I know that never again will
I have to mother a worthless shit like you. Back to your
gutter! (*Throws the diary at him.*) Kenneth was
over-reacting again today.

JOE: The gutter's for you—along with the refuse of the
modern world.
(*Rushes through some slides.*)
See this? This is just the beginning . . .

KENNETH: Of a very short fuse which, when it ignites the
powder, will explode with all the ferocity of a fat
fishwife's fart.

JOE: I didn't say my future wouldn't be controversial.

KENNETH: Future? A commercial dramatist whose creativity relies upon the hardness of his chubby cock? You can't even think up a title by yourself and that's in there. I supply all the words and you type them out.

JOE: This is not like you to venture into the future—all your glories lie in the past in a couple of prissy, provincial press cuttings. You're stepping on thin ice, Kenneth.

KENNETH: I'll survive you.

JOE: With friends to shout at—you'll have no friends when I go.

KENNETH: Keep them.

JOE: You should get a pink-rinsed poodle, they're absolutely *de rigueur* for spent pansies.

KENNETH: At least it would return the affection I gave it. Ladies and gentlemen, when we asked one hundred members of the theatre-going public how they spelt the word 'shit' they answered J . . . O . . . E . . . O . . . R . . . T . . . O . . . N and they each receive two free tickets to walk out of his next West End production entitled '*CAPSTAN . . . Can a Prick Stand Twice a Night?*'

JOE: Marvellous. How you sad nonentities can come out with things like that, apparently straight off the tops of your miserably toupéed heads, never fails to make me laugh—with embarrassment.

KENNETH: (*Swinging a blow*) I hate you.

JOE: (*Catching the arm and twisting it*) And I hate you too, darling. The adrenalin rush of violence excites me. How does it feel from your side? Do you like it?
(*Tightens grip.*)
I've just about had enough, Kenneth.

KENNETH: Get off.

JOE: What's the magic word?

KENNETH: You bastard.

JOE: That's not very wonder-working.
(*Twists further.*)

KENNETH: Please . . . ah! . . . please!

74

JOE: (*Pushing him away*) Let's just calm down a bit now, all right?
(KENNETH *swings another blow*)
I could kill you, Kenneth. But I won't. It's too easy. Your suffering would be over before I was even sentenced and I want you to suffer, believe me, I want you to suffer. How do you fancy a bit of spanky-spanky with a crowbar?

KENNETH: Homosexual playwright batters boyfriend. Theatrical world stunned. Orton's career in ruins.
(*The lights fade on them and rise on* MISS MILLIGAN's *room.* RUSSELL *and* WATSON *finish reading the diary.*)

WATSON: I'm only surprised it didn't happen sooner.

RUSSELL: That's not a diary—more of a Domesday Book.

WATSON: It's all right from Orton's point of view, after all; it's his diary, he's entitled to confide in it, that's what it's there for. Halliwell shouldn't have read it.
(*Slight pause.*)
You'd never read my diary, would you?

RUSSELL: No, of course not.
(*Thinks about it.*)
Why, what have you written about me?

WATSON: Nothing. It's personal, that's all. A diary: it's private.

RUSSELL: No, come on, what have you written?

WATSON: Russell.

RUSSELL: You've obviously written something or you'd let me read it.

WATSON: I haven't asked to read yours.

RUSSELL: I haven't got one.

WATSON: There you are then.

RUSSELL: I let you write down what happens to us.

WATSON: You're getting paranoid.

RUSSELL: You've written something nasty about me, I know what you're like.

WATSON: I haven't.

RUSSELL: What about me wanting to borrow your car?

WATSON: You have read it!

RUSSELL: You shouldn't have left it on the desk.

WATSON: That's my bloody diary.

RUSSELL: It wasn't me who messed up your stretch covers.

WATSON: What I wrote in there was for my own benefit—between me and myself.

RUSSELL: And that Polynesian bird from the chip shop. Wouldn't touch her with your barge-pole, you said to me. Funny skin and bits of fish between her teeth, you said. Didn't stop you from underlining it in red, did it? You bastard.

WATSON: Sod you, Russell, that's my diary.

RUSSELL: And I thought we were mates!

WATSON: I thought we were mates. What else have you done then? What other private and personal items of mine have you run your grubby fingers through? Thanks a bunch, pal, I won't trust you again.

RUSSELL: I won't trust *you* again.

(TRUSCOTT *enters*.)

TRUSCOTT: All right, all right, what is all this noise? I'm trying to interrogate people next door, I can hardly hear myself think let alone poke holes in their stories.

WATSON: Sorry.

TRUSCOTT: I should think so too. Have you no respect for the dead? You'll probably wake them up with your carry-on. Where's the woman?

RUSSELL: She's getting changed.

TRUSCOTT: What the hell for? Is she going to a party?

RUSSELL: She wanted to look nice for us.

TRUSCOTT: Then she'll need a plastic surgeon and Christian bloody Dior in there with her. And (*to* RUSSELL) who said you could smoke in here?

RUSSELL: No one, sir.

(TRUSCOTT *takes the cigarette from him and deliberately grinds it under his foot*.)

TRUSCOTT: You can enjoy the fag afterwards. (*Mocking*)
Have *you* solved the crime yet, constable?

RUSSELL: No sir.

TRUSCOTT: You?

(WATSON *shakes his head.*)
I thought not. *You've* been lolling about devising fanciful
theories. (*Voice rising*) It takes a hammer! . . .
(*He smacks his fist into his palm.*)
. . . to nail the criminal.
(*Quietly, indicating himself*) A hammer.
(*He eyes them, suddenly*) Attention!
(*They leap to attention. He circles.*)
Nice . . . nice . . . (*Hard command*) I expect to see the
woman when her face is dry.
(TRUSCOTT *exits.*)

WATSON: Now see what you've done, you idiot.

RUSSELL: Oh, shut up. If it weren't for your lust for fame and
fortune, we could have been enjoying ourselves and none
of this would have happened.

WATSON: I didn't kill them.

RUSSELL: Just wanted to write your thesis about them, that's
all.

WATSON: (*Calling*) Miss Milligan. We're going to a party.
(*The lights fade on them and rise on* GENZIANI's *room.*
TRUSCOTT *enters.*)

TRUSCOTT: Right, where were we?

SMART: You were fondling my cheek.

TRUSCOTT: I was checking for tightening of the muscles:
you're as flaccid as a marshmallow.

SMART: I tell you, it's a medical mystery why I seize up when
I get a shock.

GENZIANI: The boy was certainly quite stiff, Inspector.

TRUSCOTT: So you say, Mr Genziani, so you say. Tut, tut, tut. I
know one of you lot did it . . . the question is: which one?

SMART: Why don't you toss a coin?

TRUSCOTT: Oi. One more like that and you'll end up with

your balls so far dropped you'll need to fly to
Australia to pick them up.

GENZIANI: I wish you wouldn't victimize the boy for his
sexuality.

SMART: I'd really like one of his kids to turn out queer.

TRUSCOTT: (*Hearing this and then, politely*) Excuse me.
(GENZIANI *steps aside, unsuspecting, and* TRUSCOTT *grabs*
SMART*'s balls and squeezes hard.*)

SMART: Ah! Get off, you bastard.

TRUSCOTT: (*Releasing him*) Hopefully that should tighten up
that jaw muscle, Mr Smart.

GENZIANI: You can't do that.

TRUSCOTT: Did you miss it? I'll do it again if you want proof.
(GENZIANI *mutters an Italian oath. The lights fade on them and
rise on the downstairs flat.* JOE *has a box to put his belongings
in.*)

KENNETH: You're going, then.

JOE: I don't make a feasibility study of my every move, but
my imminent departure would appear to be on the
cards.

KENNETH: Well, Islington will be sorry to see you go, Noel
Road especially. They'll all mourn your passing, and the
sighs of regret from the public lavatories will fill
ammoniac air. There won't be a dry eye in the house—if
you know what I mean! Still, I'm sure we can find
another second-rate scandal-monger to move in.
(*Pause.*)
I believe the cushions are yours.

JOE: Keep them for barricading the door when the real world
pops round for a chat.

KENNETH: Half the walls are yours.

JOE: That rubbish? Save it for putting on the floor when your
poodle pisses on the lino. Uncreative and
uncommercial—who wants collages?

KENNETH: They're as viable an art form as your plays.

JOE: Cobblers. A pastiche of watery colours and the products

78

of a puerile imagination. Who attended that abortion of an exhibition?

KENNETH: Lots of people.

JOE: I actually had to beg my friends to go. My own friends! And the thought of having to buy any of the damn things made them visibly shudder.

KENNETH: At least I haven't sacrificed my artistic integrity.

JOE: Integrity! The watchword of the eternally mediocre.

KENNETH: (*Sweeping this aside and waltzing*) Don't you find this division of property a lark? I must say though that I never realized how very few things you actually possess. The skin balms and baby lotions are yours although Christ knows who you're trying to deceive—you've the complexion of a pickled walnut—and those chest expander things are yours. This is much more fun than watching you type all night or perhaps you don't agree. Do you agree, Joe? Do you, dear?

JOE: If I weren't so 'physical' I could almost entertain feelings of worry and concern for you at this moment.

KENNETH: Don't worry about me, Orton, we're finished—no ties, no nothing: remember? Sixteen years out of the window but are we downhearted? No, are we fuck. Happy to find you, happy to lose you—it must be the best way.

JOE: The best way would be for you to close your eyes and go to sleep.

KENNETH: I can't sleep.

JOE: When you wake up I shall be gone. You'll be found huddled in the corner like a frightened rabbit and there will be *The Boy Hairdresser* clasped to your palpitating heart as you sob quietly of the greatest piece of fiction ever left unpublished. Only it's not fiction, is it, Kenneth? That sad and badly written tale is your life.

KENNETH: So, from tomorrow morning I will not be seeing you again.

JOE: Not, as they say, if I see you first.

KENNETH: Just your name in lights above the annual success.

JOE: Fingers crossed.

KENNETH: I shall expect tickets to each première in mute acknowledgement of your unpaid debt.

JOE: You can come by all means, but if I hear one word of criticism from those sagging jowls of yours, I shall have no hesitation in rendering you horizontal.

KENNETH: Violence becomes you. It goes with your hair.

JOE: It could hardly go with yours.

KENNETH: What a fine profile you have . . . that sloping forehead, the heavy eyebrows, the twisted lips: Piltdown Man. I bet you even slurp your primordial soup.

JOE: It's not a joke any more, Kenneth.

KENNETH: Ug!

JOE: Primitive man lived only to satisfy his daily desires. He wasn't particularly interested in integrity or love; he only wanted to live. If I can't live because some paranoid parasite won't let me . . .

KENNETH: You're spitting.

JOE: I have to release my energy in some other way like writing.

KENNETH: Or sex.

JOE: Or sex!

KENNETH: What rubbish you come out with.

JOE: But if I can't write because a limp prick like you won't let me, then I start to hit and break things—things like this useless arm.

(*Grabs* KENNETH's *arm and twists*)

KENNETH: You've never been this butch with me before, this could be the start of a beautiful relationship.

JOE: If it weren't the end of one.

KENNETH: Go, go you bastard, you're hurting me.

JOE: Physical people hurt the mental people by ripping their arms off and hiding their pain-killers. Your brand of verbal violence is about as effective as a piss up the bum. Sticks and stones break bones!

(*Pushes* KENNETH *away. He sees the hammer on the bookcase and grabs it.*)

What's this doing out? Are you doing your messianic carpenter trick again?

(JOE *threatens him with the hammer.*)

Well?

KENNETH: You would, wouldn't you?

JOE: Try me and find out.

(*He swings the hammer menacingly.* KENNETH *takes a step backwards.* JOE *takes a step forward. He keeps swinging the hammer.*)

You're a sick man, Kenneth, they'd believe me. He went for me, I shall say, I had to defend myself. My life or his.

(*Another step forward, another step back.*)

You were like a maniac, Kenneth. If I hadn't wrenched the hammer from your hands that would have been my lot. I'll get you a wreath though—no hard feelings, eh?

(*The hammer is swinging before* KENNETH'S *eyes.* JOE *breaks into a rich laugh and turns his back on* KENNETH. KENNETH *reaches for his tablet jar and swallows several.*)

More? You'd better be careful. Come on, get a grip on yourself. You've only got another six hundred to last you the week.

(*He laughs again and tosses the hammer away. He resumes his packing by the bookcase.*)

KENNETH: Make sure none of my books go in there.

JOE: You may rest assured that I'm only taking that which is legally mine. I'm not going to be hounded by you on the pretext that I have one of your worthless paperbacks.

(*He picks up a particularly tatty book.*)

Look, Kenneth, just like you . . . spineless!

KENNETH: You are singularly arrogant and unfeeling.

JOE: I know, it's half my charm.

KENNETH: The other half of which is in residence in any one of a thousand unwashed arses.

JOE: It's called meeting one's public.

KENNETH: Leave now or I'll call the police.

(JOE *looks at him in disbelief. He laughs.*)

JOE: No one cares what happens to us, Kenneth, only you. I shall be gone in the morning and that will be quite soon enough, I'm sure.

KENNETH: Where would you go? Who would have you?

JOE: Who would I have you mean. Does it matter?

KENNETH: No.

JOE: Then shut up and keep your beady eyes on me in case I take a shine to one of your cheap toys.

KENNETH: Leave me alone.

JOE: I seriously intend to. Here, catch. You'll be needing it.
(*Throws the phallus.*)

KENNETH: You bastard. You bastard, I hate you!

JOE: Look at you—your eyes flashing like a Medea who's not going anywhere.

KENNETH: I taught you Euripides.

JOE: But I reworked him.

KENNETH: Get fucked.

JOE: A splendid idea but I don't have a penny on me. Lend us a quid.
(*He dips into* KENNETH*'s jar and flicks a tablet at him.*)
Art thou real, my ideal? With drugs like these on the market I can almost believe in Nirvana outside Morocco. I could go and live there.

KENNETH: It should suit you perfectly.

JOE: (*Cheerfully*) Yes, it should, shouldn't it? But what about you?

KENNETH: Don't bother yourself.

JOE: I must though, Ken. Sixteen years is a long time. It can't be thrown away like empty medicine bottles.

KENNETH: Why don't you leave me alone? You've won.

JOE: Religion, there's the answer. You could become a Trappist if you could keep your mouth shut. Yes, it would suit you: all the Latin you're so fond of, plus the

benefit of unnatural practices in the solitary calm of
the cloister. God looks down, gives His blessing and if you
feel guilty there's always a wank in the confessional. In
Heaven all the queers become cherubs with consecrated
genitals—Heaven indeed. You'd be a bride of Christ, I
suppose. God is a blond—he prefers gentlemen.
(*Pause.*)

KENNETH: This is it, is it?

JOE: Pushed a little too hard this evening, didn't we, Ken?

KENNETH: I feel terrible.

JOE: Kenneth, you look terrible. Cheer up, mate, it's all your
own work!
(*There is a knock at the door.* KENNETH *looks up, scared.*)
Who have we here?

KENNETH: (*Panic*) Don't open it.

JOE: (*Puzzled by the fear*) What?

KENNETH: Don't open it. I don't want to know who's there.

JOE: It could be important.

KENNETH: No.

JOE: What's wrong with you?

KENNETH: I don't want to know who's there.

JOE: Who the hell do you think it's going to be? The Grim
Reaper? Don't be so stupid.

KENNETH: (*Barring his way to the door*) No!

JOE: (*Pushing him aside*) Get out of the way.
(*He opens the door.*)
Mr Genziani, good evening.

GENZIANI: (*In dressing-gown*) Good evening to you.

JOE: (*Instantly charming*) What can we do for you?

GENZIANI: I popped down to ask whether you'd care to come
upstairs for a drink. Is everything all right?

JOE: Yes, everything's fine.

GENZIANI: It's an inconvenient moment. Sorry.

JOE: Kenneth's tired and I've got a few things to be getting
on with . . . one of the perils of the job, unfortunately . . .
and, well, I don't think we'd be very good company this

evening.

GENZIANI: No, no, quite, I just thought I'd ask.

JOE: Thanks all the same.

GENZIANI: I'll say goodnight, gentlemen, and get drunk on my own.

(*He smiles.*)

Goodnight, Kenneth.

(KENNETH *says nothing.*)

Goodnight, Joe.

JOE: Night, Charles. (*Confiding*) He's on his last legs.

GENZIANI: (*As the door closes*) Goodnight.

(*The door is closed.*)

JOE: What the hell is wrong with you?

(KENNETH *says nothing.*)

Not only do you make yourself look stupid, you make me look stupid: a ridiculous display. I've had about enough, I really have. The sooner the world knows of the end of our *ménage* the better. (*Suddenly angry again*) That's really pissed me off. *Really* pissed me off. What a way to carry on. I'm going to tell him. I'm going straight up there now and I'm going to tell him. I'm going to tell him exactly what it's about. I don't mind it when we keep it between the two of us but when you make a pratt of me in front of other people, that's too fucking much.

(*He throws open the door.*)

KENNETH: Joe.

JOE: What?

KENNETH: I still love you.

JOE: Pitiful.

(*He goes. Moments later he bursts back in—frightened and frightening.*)

'Cursed Iarbus, die to expiate
The grief that tires upon thine inward soul!—
Dido, I come to thee.—Ay me, Aeneas!'

(*Kills himself and slumps to the floor. He relishes the silence before he laughs. He sits up.*)

Love me, Kenneth? You *must* be mad.

(*The door is kicked open as* WATSON, *at one end, and* RUSSELL, *at the other, carry in the body of Joe.*)

I'm going to bed.

WATSON: That's precisely where we're taking you, Mr Orton.

(*But* JOE *has neither seen them nor heard them.*

The lights fade on them and rise on TRUSCOTT, SMART *and* GENZIANI. MISS MILLIGAN *enters.*)

TRUSCOTT: Ah, madam, come in the welcome.

MILLIGAN: (*With a twirl*) How do I look?

TRUSCOTT: Like a martyr to the menopause.

(*He waits for them to settle.*)

(*Expansive*) Who dunnit?

(*Walking past each in turn.*)

Was it the wrinkled succubus, Miss Milligan? Or the incubus in rawhide himself, Richard—'Dickie' Smart? Or was it (*Simply*) Charles Genziani, esquire? Who was capable? Who is culpable? (*Running these smoothly together.*) If you want to solve the crime, ask a policeman. (*And he chuckles at this.*) The law may be an ass, but we must pin the tail of Justice to it—and I shall not rest until this case is solved. (*Amiably*) I am reminded of the notorious nigger-in-the-woodpile murders. Those minstrels led me a merry dance I can tell you. I mention this because this case has seen me dancing once again. I do not like to dance. I tread on people's toes.

(*He produces the note from his pocket.*)

But we have been spared my more painful Terpsichorean clumsiness by, of all things, this. 'If you read this all will be explained.' (*Dismissive*) A shopping list. Tomatoes, onions, mince, pasta . . . the ingredients of spaghetti bolognese. I wonder . . .

(*This has all been to lull them into the highly favoured false sense of security. He turns quickly on* SMART . . .)

You! Where does spaghetti bolognese come from?

SMART: Tins.

(*This earns him a cuff around the ear.*)

MILLIGAN: It comes from Italy.

TRUSCOTT: Thank you, madam. And can you also tell us from where Mr Genziani comes?

MILLIGAN: Upstairs?

TRUSCOTT: No.

MILLIGAN: Leighton Buzzard?

TRUSCOTT: Slightly before that.

SMART: Italy.

TRUSCOTT: It's a small world, isn't it.

(*To* GENZIANI) You didn't happen to see Mr Orton and Mr Halliwell at any point yesterday evening?

GENZIANI: As a matter of fact I did.

(TRUSCOTT *chooses this moment to light his pipe.* GENZIANI *is forced to continue.*)

I came down and asked them whether they'd care to have a drink with me.

TRUSCOTT: And did they?

GENZIANI: No. Joe was working on something and Kenneth seemed very tired. I didn't intrude since they were both very much on edge.

TRUSCOTT: On the edge of death, if I may make so bold.

GENZIANI: With the benefit of hindsight, maybe so, yes. They certainly had been arguing.

TRUSCOTT: Argue a lot did they?

GENZIANI: Well, they certainly weren't the quietest of couples and the noise did travel some nights. And the typewriter of course. Drumming.

TRUSCOTT: Did that annoy you?

GENZIANI: One gets used to it eventually.

TRUSCOTT: Not annoyed as such.

GENZIANI: Not as such.

TRUSCOTT: But you often heard them.

GENZIANI: On occasions.

TRUSCOTT: Last night?

GENZIANI: I heard something.

TRUSCOTT: An argument?

GENZIANI: A call.

TRUSCOTT: What about the typewriter?

GENZIANI: Joe did do some typing.

TRUSCOTT: When he wasn't arguing.

GENZIANI: I didn't hear them arguing.

TRUSCOTT: But you heard a call.

GENZIANI: I heard something.

TRUSCOTT: And you asked them up for a drink.

GENZIANI: It seemed like a good idea.

TRUSCOTT: So you could find out what all the noise was about.

GENZIANI: I was mildly curious.

TRUSCOTT: But they refused your hospitality.

GENZIANI: They did.

TRUSCOTT: And so you killed them.

GENZIANI: No!

SMART: (*An imaginary gong.*) Bong!

GENZIANI: (*Checking his watch*) Inspector, much as I admire the work you're doing here, I am a busy man and I do have a previous engagement . . .
(*He begins to go.*)

TRUSCOTT: (*Pleasantly*) One moment please, Charles. I must warn you that if you set one foot outside that door, it will be quite within my powers as an agent of justice and an affiliate member of the Metropolitan Water Board to have you stood up against a wall and hosed down. I'm afraid. (*He smiles.*)

GENZIANI: (*Forced to stay*) You know I didn't do it.

SMART: Why should he? They were neighbours.

TRUSCOTT: That's exactly it, though. The noise they made travelled directly upwards.

GENZIANI: (*Dry*) Thank you, Richard.

TRUSCOTT: Typing all hours, the cacophony of homosexual life . . . it's enough to get on anybody's tits.

GENZIANI: People don't get killed because of the noise they
make.

TRUSCOTT: They often get killed for a lot less.

GENZIANI: Can you really be so stupid?

TRUSCOTT: I can do anything if I apply my mind to it.

MILLIGAN: But Mr Genziani is an impeccable tenant—he isn't
a murderer.

TRUSCOTT: Oh no? How many have you met?

MILLIGAN: (*Meekly*) Well . . . he doesn't look like one.

TRUSCOTT: You wouldn't recognize a murderer if he smashed
your brains out. But why should I listen to you—to any
of you? You can't even shed a tear for them. Okay, they
were a pair of old irons but people cry over dead dogs. If
that'd been Lassie and Rin-Tin-Tin callously
despatched, you'd have been howling your bloody eyes
out.

GENZIANI: Surely, Inspector, the whole case is tragically clear:
Kenneth killed Joe as the result of some serious mental
imbalance and then took his own life by a drug
overdose.

TRUSCOTT: Suicide? Mr Genziani, everyone knows the
suicidal want sympathy and attention. Mr Halliwell
could hardly expect his companion to lend him a
friendly ear—especially considering that by this time the
said friendly ear is bloodily hanging off, courtesy of a
number of blows to the head administered by Mr
Halliwell. No, I'm sorry Charles, but all the evidence
seems to point to you . . .

GENZIANI: I cannot cope with this moronic logic. If I'd done
that to them, would I still be here now?

TRUSCOTT: Popular criminology asserts that the villain will
always return to the scene of his crime.

MILLIGAN: He does live here.

TRUSCOTT: Irrelevant!

MILLIGAN: You didn't do it, did you?

GENZIANI: No, Miss Milligan, I did not do it. This is a

88

contortion of the facts.

TRUSCOTT: I prefer 'an aesthetic arrangement' in keeping with the Force's fine reputation for beauty and truth. I've got to balance the books, tidy everything away . . . a crime has been committed—no question of that—and someone has to take the blame.

(*He produces handcuffs.*)

Come on Charlie-boy.

GENZIANI: I most strongly protest.

TRUSCOTT: Of course you do.

SMART: If you've arrested him, does that mean I can go?

TRUSCOTT: (*Ignoring* SMART *and fitting cuffs.*) The bitter irony of it is, Charles, that if it weren't for you and your mates none of this would have happened, do you know what I mean? 'I'll have one half of bitter beer and what oppressed minority shall we bring out from the woodwork? Let's bring the pouftahs out today, shall we Tom? Good idea.' You can't go into a public convenience any more without getting approached— pissing has become this country's largest spectator sport. No, you say, these people have rights just like any other normal, decent, hard-working citizen. And all well and good . . . until a pair of them happen to move into the same house as you! Then what happens? The typing starts. You can't sleep at night because the air is rent with the sounds of sodomy. The value of your property plummets. Friends make excuses rather than come round for tea. The stair carpet gets worn away by the constant traffic of stilettos. All good mitigating circumstances, Charles, you'll probably only get a couple of years. Lucky for you they abolished the death sentence, eh?

(*A knock on the door.* WATSON *enters.*)

WATSON: We're ready sir.

TRUSCOTT: Excellent. I've arranged a little reconstruction, Charles, now that the administration is out of the way. I want you to see what I'm nicking you for.

(*The lights fade on them and rise on the downstairs flat.* KENNETH *stands above* JOE *with the hammer gripped in his hand.* RUSSELL *is just making sure that he is in the correct position—he straightens* KENNETH's *pyjamas, tips the hammer to a nice angle, etc.*)

RUSSELL: Did he always sleep with his mouth open? He looks very peaceful. Anyway, Kenneth, as I was saying, we're very like-minded men. Caught up in events and so forth. Nobody understands, do they? I mean, WE understand but it's the others you've got to worry about. You're a fascinating man, did you know that?

(*He checks the corpse of* KENNETH *which is now as it was earlier.*)

Is this how we found you, Kenneth? It was all so much of a rush that I can't remember whether you were lying this way or that way. Still, I don't suppose it really matters. Are you relaxed?

(KENNETH *neither moves nor says anything.*)

Well, here we are . . . the moments before you killed him. How does it feel? What's going through your mind right now? If you've anything you want to say you'd better say it before the others come down. All right for tablets? I've put out the grapefruit juice to wash them down. You don't mind if I talk, do you? I'm just trying to work out what's going through your mind.

(*He falls into silence.*)

I'm getting a bit tense, myself. Won't be long now. Just keep telling yourself he deserved it, something like that.

(*The door opens.*)

Aah.

(*With relief*) Here they are.

TRUSCOTT: Mr Orton opens the door and you say. . . ?

GENZIANI: Would you care to come upstairs for a drink?

TRUSCOTT: Now that's not what you said, is it? More along the line of 'You bloody queers, can't you keep the noise

90

down, there's a fair-minded liberal next door who
needs his eight hours!'
(*They all troop into the room.*)
This is what the jury likes to hear. They'll probably be
very sympathetic Charles . . . suspended sentence?

GENZIANI: Tell him, Kenneth, tell him it wasn't me.

RUSSELL: Please, this is a very emotional moment for Mr
Halliwell.

MILLIGAN: (*With a shy wave*) Hello, Kenneth.
(*Aside to* SMART) I thought he was dead.
(*To* KENNETH) You're not dead, are you, Kenneth?

TRUSCOTT: Shut up, woman. Is he ready?

RUSSELL: I think so.

TRUSCOTT: In your own time, Mr Halliwell.

GENZIANI: Don't do it, Kenneth.

WATSON: Objection!

TRUSCOTT: Sustained. Silence in court. One more like that,
Genziani, and I'll have your tongue out.
(*They all watch* KENNETH. *He does not move.* SMART *and*
WATSON *begin to get restless.*)

SMART: (*An impatient mutter*) Get on with it.

MILLIGAN: Would you like another cup of tea, Kenneth?

RUSSELL: Shush, he's concentrating.
(*By way of encouragement*) This is truly fascinating.
(*They wait again.* WATSON *looks at his watch.*)

TRUSCOTT: Don't force me to charge you with wasting police
time.

SMART: He's not going to do it, he's spineless.

GENZIANI: Don't listen to them, Kenneth. Give the man a
chance, Richard.

TRUSCOTT: I sincerely hope we haven't been brought here
under false pretences. Constable?

WATSON: He'll do it—he's gone beyond the point of no
return.
(SMART, *bored, plays with the slide projector. Slides flash up.*)

GENZIANI: Kenneth, listen to me. There's no such thing as the

91

point of no return. You can stop. You can turn
back. Maybe everything will be all right in the morning.

WATSON: It won't be. Every card he's played has been
trumped. He's got nothing to turn back to. He's
finished.

MILLIGAN: He can always have a cup of tea with me.

TRUSCOTT: If that's all that's on offer he might as well do it.

(*A slide of* KENNETH *minus his wig.*)

SMART: (*Laughing*) Look at him! What a dome-head! Christ,
what did Joe see in him?

(*The others begin to laugh with him.*)

You couldn't get famous looking like that. Stand him by
a road and people would think he was a Belisha beacon.
No talent . . . no style . . . no personality . . . and no
bloody hair!

(*They are all looking at the slide now. Looking and laughing.*)

KENNETH: (*Screams*) No!

(*The lights go out. The projector clicks on but there are no more
slides.* JOE *wakes and half rises.*)

JOE: (*Sleepily*) Kenneth, if you're going to nail yourself to a
cross, can you do it quietly?

(KENNETH *raises the hammer.*)

BLACKOUT